LAMBS OF THE LIE

A NOVEL

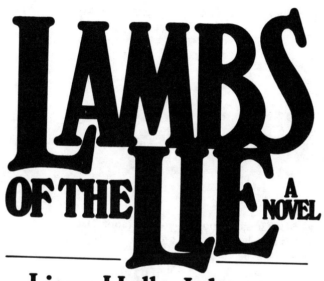

LAMBS OF THE LIE

A NOVEL

Lissa Halls Johnson

Power Books

Fleming H. Revell Company
Old Tappan, New Jersey

Scripture quotations in this volume are author's paraphrase of the King James Version of the Bible.

Library of Congress Cataloging-in-Publication Data
Johnson, Lissa Halls, date.
   Lambs of the lie.

   I. Title.
PS3560.037975L3 1987   813'.54   87-9658
ISBN 0-8007-5251-1

Copyright © 1987 by Lissa Halls Johnson
Published by the Fleming H. Revell Company
Old Tappan, New Jersey 07675
Printed in the United States of America

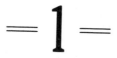

=T he ambulance screamed for room to streak down the boulevard through the night. Two blocks away, Deanna shoved up the window, hoping the layers of paint wouldn't make it stick again. The wood squeaked a protest, then gave way with a jerk. She pressed her nose against the screen. She knew a little, black waffle mark was being pressed into it, and she didn't care. She strained to see the stars, but the street light on the sidewalk in front of the house stole them away.

The night was not cold, but Deanna was chilled by the confusion, frustration, and total loneliness that covered her like the night. It didn't help that the noise of the city kept her awake.

The first time Deanna saw this house, it looked to her much like the other wooden sideboard houses in Los Angeles, except that it was painted green instead of white. It did have the standard green lawn, like an apron skirting around the house. The old, cracked driveway slid alongside the house to a crooked garage, pushed to the back of the property.

The windows, all large with four square panes in each, were the eyes of the occupants on the world outside. The inside had been renovated recently—new carpets, paint, and drapes. The kitchen, too, had a face-lift, stacked with new cabinets, adorned with new tile, but still as small as an afterthought.

It didn't really matter to Deanna how the house looked at all. Even if it had been a mansion, she still would have longed for her big childhood home in La Crescenta.

La Crescenta, only twenty minutes away if her dad drove slowly, which wasn't likely, was a world away in every other consideration. The foothills were quiet and smogless for most of the year. Her home happened to be set back from the street at the end of a long driveway. Not a fancy house. Just real old and real big, with memories popping joyfully out of every crack. Even some of the rocks held memories for the Clark family: memories of bumped knees and bonked heads—one bad enough to need five stitches.

The fragrant pine trees made a small forest in front.

Two big, fat tears rolled down her cheeks as Deanna scanned the street. It wasn't as if she belonged in La Crescenta, either. But at least she had a few friends there to hang around with. Low riders crept by, their radios blaring songs in Spanish, dark-haired heads on bodies sunk low in the seats. Other cars raced by, with Deanna wondering how they could squeeze by each other and between parked cars without hitting something.

It was scary here—scary because crime was a little higher. Violent crimes happened far more often. She knew that because her mother kept pointing out all the newspaper articles to her father, never saying a word.

But more frightening than the crime was the starting over, the not belonging. She was always the one on the outside looking in. Would she ever fit in anywhere? She had thought she had a chance in La Crescenta, but not here.

"Why do we have to move?" Deanna had asked them one Saturday morning during breakfast. The sun streamed through the open windows, the pine smell sweeping in with the trills of the songbirds.

Deanna's mom looked out the window and sighed. "I hate to leave this place too," she said sadly. With conviction, she added, "We don't need this big house anymore now that your sisters are all gone. And with two in college, we need more cash to support them. It made more sense to move to a smaller house."

"Why couldn't you find a smaller house nearby?"

The newspaper rustled to the table as her father answered. "The homes here are almost twice as much as those in Eagle Rock. To cut back, you have to make some sacrifices."

"Will we still go to our church?"

Mrs. Clark looked at her husband. He seemed to ignore the look and leaned back in his chair. "Deanna, you know that for the past year, ever since the new man came to pastor, we have had difficulty with his funny ideas."

Deanna rolled her eyes. She stood, picked up her chair and slammed it to the floor. "You keep talking about these 'funny ideas,' but you never let me know what they are."

Mrs. Clark put a timid hand on Deanna's shoulder. "It's not necessary for you to know, honey."

"Mom, I'm sixteen. I can handle a few funny ideas."

Mr. Clark picked up the paper and snapped it open. "End of discussion, Deanna. We have had more experience in this area than you."

Now, as Deanna looked into the night, she mimicked softly, " 'We've had more experience in this area than you.' Whenever you don't know what you're talking about you always say that, Dad." She wished she could say it to his face, but she had never been very brave. She had never been very *anything*. Just there.

She hated living in the shadow of her sisters. They all had done well in school. Not top students, but well enough to make any parent proud. Two were going to college. The oldest had graduated in June, and she already had a good job.

Deanna turned away from the window. She looked around at the pristine room, decorated just the way her mom liked it and Deanna hated it. The pink dotted swiss bedspread lay on the paint-chipped and gouged canopy bed. The ancient bedspread was a hand-me-down from sister number two. It belonged on a six-year-old's bed, not a sixteen-year-old's.

Each time Deanna complained about it, her mom would tell her, "It was fine for your sister; it will be fine for you. You need something feminine in your life. Something lacy and frilly."

She pulled back the covers and lay down on the bed. Her request for a shade to block out the street light was met with another standard answer. "We can't afford it." Oh, how she hated those words!

She lay down on the cool sheets, pulling the thin blanket up to her chin. She faced the wall, and saw her shadow. She talked to her shadow, feeling completely foolish, but wanting someone to talk to. "Is there something wrong and unfeminine about liking old-fashioned quilts and furniture? Mother thinks so. If it doesn't have *prissy* written all over it, it's not feminine. I'm so tired of her wanting me to be like my sisters."

She flopped on her back and stared at the delicate bows, their pink ends cascading over the sides of the canopy. "I only want someone to like me for who I am. Pooh! It's awful being the tail end of a line of sisters. They've done it all before, said it all before, been clever enough before so that I can't say or do anything new. If I do, it's unacceptable because it doesn't follow the norm."

Deanna flopped over once more and then got out of bed. She pulled a stool up to the window and sat on it, her chin in her hands, while her elbows rested on the gritty ledge. She stared and thought until her eyes got droopy. She thought about church and talking to God. She looked up into the dark sky. "God, is it too much to ask that somebody somewhere like me for what I am? I know I'm a little different than a lot of the kids. I'm not good-looking enough to be a cheerleader, I've started school mid-semester; I'm a whiz at math, but such a dunce in everything else that I'll never make it to college—or at least past junior college. Can't You send somebody who thinks my words are clever sometimes, and my ideas worth listening to?"

After her awkward prayer, she smiled and chuckled at herself. "What a dummy. I've had friends before. Maybe it was just warm-up for the real good friends I've always dreamed about."

She dropped in her bed and closed her eyes so she wouldn't have to see the pink glow that her bed and the streetlight together made.

*   *   *

Jeff stuffed his books into the worn, khaki backpack. He pulled the straps through the bindings and cinched them tight. He looked in the mirror, running a comb through his sandy-brown curls one more time. He fastened his watch and headed down the stairs.

Walking through the kitchen, he kissed his mom on the cheek. "Bye, Mom. See you at four."

"Are you going to Flock tonight?"

"Yeah. If Cramer doesn't load up on the trig homework. Shep says trig is more important than Flock."

Melinda set down her coffee mug. "I love that man. He is so wise." She reached up to poke Jeff's arm. "He also keeps my best son in line."

"Your only son, Mom."

"Hmm. Well. You'd still probably be my best son, even if you weren't the only one."

Jeff touched her shoulder. "Thanks anyway, even if I don't believe it."

A concerned look passed over Melinda's face. "Jeff," she said, then paused. "I heard someone say the Flock is a cult." Her voice ended on a high note, almost as if she were asking a question.

Jeff smiled. "They sure don't know what they're talking about, do they, Mom?"

Melinda smiled back, confidence returning. "No, honey, they don't. Have a good day at school."

Jeff kissed her lightly on the forehead and flung the backpack over one shoulder. He skipped all four front steps and headed toward school. Jeff couldn't get his mind off the new girl who transferred to Central High two weeks ago. She was so different from the other girls. He never told anyone, because he knew it could sound conceited, but he got tired of girls flirting with him.

Shep encouraged him to be friendly, and let the love of Christ shine through him, so that more could taste the sweetness of salvation. But Jeff knew that the minute he smiled at one of them, they all seemed to swoon. He hated it. It made the other guys at school not like him. He was in on the competition and he didn't want to be.

Jeff looked over his shoulder at the approaching, honking car and waved at the occupants as they flew by. He didn't mind not being a part of the groups at school. He wanted it that way. The Flock encouraged him to live in the world without being a part of it.

His mom had looked at him with surprise when he asked if they could get rid of the television and cancel the subscription to the newspaper. He explained Shep encouraged it so they could keep their minds focused on the more important aspects of life.

His mother agreed to the TV finding a new home, but his father put his foot down, right on top of the newspaper, and said it stayed. He reluctantly agreed to read and keep it in his bedroom so Jeff would not see it.

Jeff stopped at the top of the stairs outside Central High, his gaze caught by the new girl. Her brown hair blew behind her when she walked. She held her notebook and stack of textbooks to her chest and studied the ground intently. When she got to the bottom of the steps, she looked to the top, her face looking like a frightened doe. *Or a lost lamb.*

"Oh, Jeff," a voice sang behind him. He turned to see Alyee coming toward him. She slid her slender hand through his crooked arm and steered him to the inside of the building. "I haven't seen you in so long. When *are* you going to take me to another concert? I just loved the way that group seemed—I don't know—so *alive*, I guess."

Jeff tried to stop the blush warming his face. "The next one is scheduled a week from Saturday. I'll be happy to take you and a few of your friends."

Alyee's face fell a little, her bottom lip poking out. "But I thought it could be just you and me, Jeff."

"Alyee," he scolded. "You know I'm very busy at those concerts. You would be all by yourself." He hated what Shep would think if he heard him talk like that. Shep wanted them to bring anyone and everyone to the concerts, to the Flock meetings. If they didn't come, how would they hear? If they didn't hear, how would they know? If they didn't know, how would they find?

But Shep doesn't know how hard it is. He demands purity, and it's hard to maintain pure thoughts when a girl like Alyee is begging for you to be impure.

Alyee's lip pushed out even farther, her daggerlike nails digging into his arm and stopping him. "Oh, Jeffie. Can't you get out of helping just once?"

Jeff felt the blush coming back. "I'm afraid I can't." He pried her fingers loose and rushed down the hall. He avoided his locker and went straight to class.

He slipped into his seat and pulled out his Spanish book. He read a story, trying to increase his speed and understanding. Languages did not come easy, but they were important—so important, he begged his counselor to let him take French as well as Spanish. He was getting a *B* in Spanish, but barely making a *C* in French. Shep would never approve.

=2=

=**D**eanna couldn't help but notice the best-looking guys in the school. She tried to look when they wouldn't notice her watching them. She scrolled her name with each one, trying to see which would look the best. She kept the papers well hidden, ripped them into tiny pieces, and threw them away with her lunch sack.

She watched to see who was available and who wasn't. It didn't look like any of the best-looking guys were un-attached. Of course not! How stupid! It was always like that. The best looking and jocks went first. The gleeps were always available. *Like me,* she thought.

The best-looking one had been standing at the top of the stairs that morning before she started up. At first she thought he was looking at her, but then scoffed at the thought. Some glamorous girl came and escorted him away. He must have been looking for her.

His eyes were a soft brown, matching his hair. He had a mouthful of braces, but smiled as if he didn't. He seemed so self-confident—like he didn't care what anyone else thought of him. His laughter bubbled out from some happy place deep inside. You could just tell.

She watched him at lunch every day as she sat under a sycamore tree. After the first week, she no longer watched him. She was too busy making friends with some of the kids who went to her new church.

The new church was okay, and the kids were nice. But she could tell she still had second-class standing. All her clothes were "nice," but out-of-date. She had to live off hand-me-downs from her sisters. The kids at her new church were dressed right, had the right answers, and played volleyball real well. Deanna never did master volleyball. She wished church kids played Ping-Pong instead. She could slaughter anyone in Ping-Pong.

"Hey, dreamy eyes, what are you thinking about?" Kathy asked, as she sat next to her on the bench.

Deanna looked up, seeing her own reflection in the glasses of her new friend. "Oh," Deanna said, trying to think of something acceptable to say. "I'm thinking about trig."

"*Blech*. What about trig?"

"I'm trying to decide if I should stay after school for an hour to start my homework before I volunteer, or go home and do the work after I volunteer."

"Hey, I didn't know you volunteer."

"Yeah, my mom got me started in it. It's real fun."

"Isn't it yucky? Don't you have to do gross things like roll over old people or wash out bedpans?"

Deanna tipped her head back and laughed. "Hardly. I volunteer at the Children's Hospital. I read books to the kids, talk to them, answer their dumb riddles, and basically play with them. It's a real kick."

"How often do you do that?"

"At least once a week. I try to go for a full day on Saturday whenever I can. Those kids really like me."

"I couldn't stand to see sick kids. It would make me cry," Kathy said as she stared at her sandwich.

"Lots of people can't stand it—but I like it. Kids have so much life, even when they're sick. It's kind of nice to make somebody who is crying, smile."

"You can have it," Kathy said, shaking her head.

Deanna thought she saw Jeff looking in her direction over the top of three girls' heads. She could have sworn he was walking their way, when Kathy grabbed her arm. "Oh, I almost forgot, I promised Linda that we'd meet her in the library. She wants you to help her with her trig."

*   *   *

The small library was anything but quiet. A group of ninth-grade boys sat at a corner table, tossing bits of broken pencil around the room. No one seemed to be studying, except a few in the very back of the library. Linda looked very confused, draped over her book with her long hair hanging in curtains on either side of her face. Wadded-up pieces of paper littered the floor around her. As Deanna and Kathy approached, Linda dabbed at her eyes with a shredded tissue.

Deanna tried not to smile. "Poor thing," she said to Kathy. "Why does she torture herself so?"

"She's got to do it for college."

Deanna slipped into the empty seat next to Linda.

"It's impossible to understand this junk," Linda wailed.

"Next to, but not impossible. Here, let me help. What question are you on?"

For the next twenty minutes, Deanna patiently explained the intricacies of trigonometry until Linda suddenly smiled. "I get it! Watch." She took the pencil and paper and began writing figures and calculating.

Deanna patted her on the back. "You'll do it. I know you will." She gathered her things and moved to her next class when the bell rang.

Kathy caught up with her. "What is that book on the top?" she asked.

Deanna blushed. "It's a Bible."

"Are you a religious nut?"

"No," Deanna said, hesitating before continuing. "I . . . I'm just looking for something. I know God has the answer, but I'm not sure what it is."

"Why do you think God has the answer?"

"Maybe because people who know Him seem to like themselves and everyone else. I don't like myself at all, and so sometimes I forget anyone else is around."

Kathy looked confused. "But you've only been here three weeks, and you're already helping everyone with trig, even though they're older than you."

Deanna bit the inside of her cheek. "But do they like me for any other reason?"

Kathy didn't answer.

"See? I'm just a nobody. I always have been. I'm a nobody at home, I'm a nobody at school, unless someone needs my mathematical brain." Deanna stopped and smiled. "I shouldn't gripe. I'll find someone who needs me, and that person will get all I've got to give. Then, watch out, World!"

Kathy laughed. "I don't doubt it. Do you think the Bible will help?"

"I know it will," Deanna said with a smile. "There is so much here of how God accepts everyone, even prostitutes."

"Maybe you ought to become one to make sure God accepts you," Kathy teased.

Deanna laughed as she opened the door to her English class. She slipped into her seat in the front row just as the tardy bell rang. In her three weeks at Central High, she had been so involved in doing her work and catching up on the required reading and assignments for the class, that she really hadn't paid attention to the other students. In trig, she felt embarrassed as one of only two juniors in the class. She still didn't know who the other one was. She made a mental note to find out the next morning.

After the tardy bell, Mr. Rodell had them number off from one to eight. All the "ones" got together in one group, all the "twos" in another, and so on. As the chairs were dragged and shoved across the pocked linoleum floor, setting up eight circles of four to five students, she came face-to-face with Jeff. He smiled and said, "Hi!"

Deanna looked behind her, certain there was someone else he spoke to. No one was there, and when she turned around to return the greeting, he had settled in the group next to hers.

*   *   *

Jeff half-listened to the plans his group made for the English project. He tried to position himself in the chair so he could see the other groups in the room. Two other kids who went to Flock meetings with him on Thursday nights were there. Their smiles were their trademark. Nothing got them down. Their devotion and responsibility were unheard of in teenagers. *After all,* Jeff thought, *teenagers are supposed to be careless and foolish. Well, not those who belong to the Flock. They have direction, purpose, strong goals, and something else,* he smiled.

"Jeff, what do you think?" Bruce asked.

Jeff smiled warmly. "Whatever you guys choose is fine with me. I'm not much of an English professor, you know."

The group laughed. As Jeff leaned back in his chair, something caught his eye. *I knew it!* his mind exclaimed. *Deanna carries a Bible.*

He yanked a piece of paper from his notebook, scribbled a quick message then folded it. He glanced around to be certain no one saw him, then let his long arm fall behind his chair. He opened the Bible with his thumb and let the note drop in.

*   *   *

The smog hung thick and heavy, clamping the heat beneath it. Deanna strolled down the main boulevard. A few times she had chosen the residential route on the way home from school. She loved to go that way whenever she felt serene and at peace, which wasn't often. It heightened her feelings of serenity when she admired the variety and sameness of the old homes—stepping over buckled sidewalks, and listening to the occasional bird call to another in the trees; smelling the eucalyptus trees, the tall palms rustling overhead. It clothed her in the stability and rigid structure she searched for.

Most days, the boulevard with its racing cars, cacophony of smells and sounds, appealed to her. Depending on which side of the street she walked, she could pass the old theater (admission still two dollars a show if you don't mind slightly gummy seats), a funeral home, and a pleasant-looking church. Gas stations, crumbling, abandoned buildings, and trash-littered parking lots lined the other side.

Her favorite place was the corner grocery store, three blocks from home. Deanna imagined it must have been there since someone decided the street belonged in that exact spot. Rusty newspaper racks leaned clumsily against the dirty, white stucco wall. High windows, black from years of dirt, lined the front of the building beyond the reach of anyone but an eight-foot giant.

Her eyes took a few moments to adjust to the dimly lit inside. She loved to wander down the crooked and sparsely stocked aisles, which carried the items any family would need at the spur of the moment.

At the back wall stood her destination—a small bakery emitting yummy, warm smells, competing with the thick blood smell of the meat counter. The gooey, warm cookies, sticky doughnuts, and cinnamon twists offered the hardest choices Deanna ever thought possible. The old baker, as soft, round, and warm as her unsliced fresh bread, seemed to save a special smile and greeting for Deanna.

The store, too, exuded belonging and stability in Deanna's jumbled-up world.

All was not bad in Deanna's world. She knew it and never claimed that it was. Life was pretty good. There were just too many adjustments to make at once, and one big hole that had to be filled.

As usual, no one awaited her after-school arrival at home. She wasn't afraid. That was absurd. She was sixteen. But sometimes she wished her mom would be home so she could talk to her and tell her about the day. She had silly dreams that her mother could sit and laugh with her over the weirdness of school and teachers, and sigh over the good-lookers.

She went to her room and dropped her books on her bed. She hadn't noticed how her Bible looked a little bulgy. *I don't remember putting anything in there.*

Her brows pulled together as she stared at the note that fell out. Reading the note, she wondered who would play such a cruel trick on her.

> Hi, I hope I'm not being rude. But I noticed your Bible. Can we talk about it? At lunch? If you say yes, I'll meet you at the green bench under the sycamore tree.

It was signed JEFF. But she knew it couldn't be true. She folded the note, started to tear it, then stopped. She opened it again and studied it.

* * *

Deanna didn't know whether to sit under the tree or not. She wondered who wrote the note, and if he, she, or they would be sitting on the balcony waiting for her to take the bait so they could have their fill of glee for the day.

On the other hand, if Jeff *had* written the note, she would be a fool to ignore it.

The next day, she grabbed her lunch from the locker and replaced it with her books. She walked a slow, casual walk out the heavy double doors into the bright sunshine. She paused at the top of the gum-spackled stairs, and shaded her eyes, looking around the crowded quad. At the bottom of the stairs, she wandered about, as if looking for a place to sit. She strolled around the quad, then happened to choose to sit on the bench under the sycamore tree.

She hoped anyone wanting to play her the fool would think she never found the note in her Bible, and by chance chose the bench suggested in the note.

She slowly opened her lunch sack and gazed into it, dreaming about Jeff, forgetting her intentions of taking out her sandwich.

"Hi," a gentle voice said, startling Deanna.

She looked up into the warm face, and tried not to let her jaw drop to the ground. "Uh, hi," she said uncertainly.

"I'm glad you came. I'm sorry I'm late. I had to do a couple things for Mr. Cramer first."

Deanna cocked her head. "Mr. Cramer?"

"Yeah. Trig."

"Are you in third period trig?"

"You didn't know?" Jeff asked, looking puzzled.

Deanna blushed. "I have been so, uh, involved in the work, I didn't even notice who else was in the class." Her lips parted into a smile. "I wondered who the other crazy junior was in the class. Where have you been hiding?"

"In the back of the class. Mr. Cramer likes me to take the chair in the back corner. He knows I'm there because I want to be. Then he doesn't have to watch for someone falling asleep or fooling around."

Deanna looked away from his piercing eyes into her lap.

She noticed she had smashed her lunch under her tightly squeezed fists.

"I . . ." Jeff sounded nervous. "I wanted to meet you."

Deanna's long lashes flashed up as she looked into his face. "You did?" she asked, incredulous.

"I noticed that you're a lot different than the other girls, and that you carry a Bible."

"Oh," she said, her gaze drifting off to the crowd. She noticed a group of four girls, including the one she saw cart Jeff away the other morning at the top of the school stairs.

"Your girlfriend is coming."

Jeff's thick brows pulled together in confusion. "My what?" He turned his head to follow her gaze. "Oh, no," he groaned.

"I'd better go, Jeff, I wouldn't want to get you in trouble or anything." Deanna scooped up her things and hurried away.

Jeff called after her, "No, Deanna. You don't understand."

"Oh, Jeffie," Deanna heard a saccharine voice say. She never turned around.

───

March 16

Three very young, very pretty, very American women, dressed in plain skirts and functional blouses, waited to board JAL's flight 079 for it's twelve-hour flight to Japan.

Behind them, tennis shoes squeaked across the linoleum corridor. Heels tic-tacked even rhythms, leather business shoes thudded with purpose and immediate goals. A baby's cry drowned the flight's final call announcement as it spluttered over the speaker.

At the other end of the sprawling Los Angeles International Airport, seven more women approached the Pan Am check-in desk to confirm seat assignments for their trip to South America. Each one, in her own hesitant manner, glanced at the television monitor. The flight would depart on schedule.

Each of the ten women kissed their "family" good-bye, choking back the tears that would be unholy. For to be sad about embarking on a mission for God would somehow say He had not been wise. None of the young women dared accuse God of being less than omniscient.

Each of the young women had similar thoughts that were unshared. About to plunge into the unknown, they were torn between duty and desire. Their duty: to serve totally their God in another land. They had learned the language well, and now would go use it to find more of the lost lambs and bring them into the fold.

The unspoken, denied desire was to remain in the comfort of sameness—in the comfort of ritual and rut; stay in the loving arms of the "family," the "Flock." But they would not question, they would not cry. They would only go and sacrifice.

Each young woman carried one small piece of luggage containing one change of clothing, nightclothes, toothbrush, soap, and other necessities. Only one carry-on bag, so there would be a quick pass through customs. They wouldn't need much. New and glorious clothes—fit for a bride—waited for them in their final destination.

No one but the Shepherd and a few of his closest assistants knew how final that destination would be.

3

="Hi, Mom!" Shawna hugged her mom and gave her a kiss on the cheek. Her greeting was followed by Dawn's and Claire's.

"Hi, everyone!" Deanna said, bounding into the room.

"Oh, hi, Deanna," they all said one at a time. As a group, they went into the living room, everyone talking at once. Deanna plopped in her favorite chair, a large, overstuffed, green monstrosity. She watched her sisters vie for her mother's attention, her mother trying to listen to everyone at once.

Deanna's dad marched in to a chorus of "Dad!" He smiled and gathered his kisses, and sat on the edge of a chair. "So," he said brightly. "How's the birthday girl?"

Claire smiled. "I'm just fine, Daddy. This is so much fun to have all of us together. Turning twenty won't be so bad after all."

Mrs. Clark patted Shawna's hand. "Come help me get the cake ready."

"Okay, Mom."

Claire faked surprise. "A cake? Really, Mom? I can't believe it. Everything is so perfect."

Deanna rolled her eyes.

"Dawn, got any hot prospects these days?" Claire asked her sister.

"There is this guy—he's positively *gorgeous*. His name is Jim. I think he's going to ask me out. At least he'd better!"

"A guy wrote me a note in school," Deanna said.

Dawn threw a disgusted look at Claire, then looked at Deanna. "Oh," she said flatly. Dawn then turned her attention back to Claire. "What about you, Claire, are you still dating Peter?"

"You bet."

"Is it serious?"

Claire glanced in her father's direction, then turned and winked at Dawn. "Maybe."

"Happy birthday to you . . ." Mrs. Clark and Shawna sang as they came in bearing a candle-laden cake. The rest of the family joined in.

*   *   *

Deanna carried the crumb-sprinkled plates to the kitchen, and brought the pot for another round of coffee, while Claire opened her gifts. She ooohed over each one, and kissed her sisters and father thanks. She opened Deanna's gift—two bottles of her favorite nail polish. "Thanks," she waved to her.

The conversation drifted from point to point—Shawna's work, school for Dawn and Claire.

"There are only two juniors in my trig class," Deanna said, trying to break into the conversation, "and I'm one of them."

"Hhm," ho-hummed Dawn, sounding more like an exhale than a response.

"Have you noticed how college work is so much more difficult than high school?" Claire asked.

Dawn nodded her agreement. "Some people think they'll be such good students, and, wham! they get to college, and it's a total shock."

Shawna looked from one sister to the other. "You'll survive."

Claire looked toward Deanna, then looked away, answering Shawna in a conspiratorial whisper. "Not everyone does, you know."

Deanna pretended she didn't hear. She curled up in the massive chair, and watched the animated faces and listened to the voices of her family. Her dad leaned forward in his chair, his hands clasped over the empty space between his knees, where his forearms rested.

"I'm going to bed," Deanna announced when she'd had enough.

"Oh, good night, honey," her mother said, then turned back to her sisters, who only waved their good nights. She kissed her dad on the cheek, who gave her a hug in return.

She closed the door to her room, and tried to close her ears to their words.

* * *

THURSDAY, MARCH 10. ALL CSF STUDENTS PLEASE MEET AT LUNCH IN ROOM ONE-FIFTEEN FOR THE MONTHLY MEETING.

Jeff closed his ears to the ritual announcements. Most bordered on absurd, none applied. He opened a small notebook, glancing over his Spanish scrawling. He shook his head and twisted his mouth. "When am I ever going to learn how to write?" he muttered.

Sheila leaned across her desk and peered over his shoulder. "Doctors write better than that."

Jeff smiled. "Thanks for the encouragement."

"Anytime, sweetie."

A bright red flush crept up Jeff's neck, swarmed over his ears and took over his cheeks. Sheila's jacket zipper clunked on her desk as she relaxed in the seat, chuckling.

ALL STUDENTS WISHING TO PURCHASE FLOWERS FOR FLOWER
DAY TOMORROW, PLEASE DO SO AT SNACK OR LUNCH.

Jeff's mind jabbed him like an elbow in his side. He
smiled. *Two flowers for every period,* he thought.

It frustrated him that he could never seem to catch
Deanna to talk to her. Two weeks of chase made him feel
foolish. He blamed it all on Alyee that Deanna avoided
him.

Jeff knew he should confess to Shep that this special girl
distracted his mind from the Word and the Work, but he
kept rationalizing that he tried to speak to her because she
might be interested in the Flock.

Jeff needed one more convert to fulfill his quota before
he could apply to become a True Lamb. He could always
get Alyee to join the Flock if he played her game long
enough. And Shep said any method used to bring someone into the Flock is holy and acceptable. But he couldn't
imagine Alyee ever becoming a True Lamb, so what was
the use? Shep would remind Jeff not to try to outguess
God.

On the other hand, Deanna had the qualities of a True
Lamb and beyond. His time would be better spent with
her.

Jeff stared at the notebook in front of him. *Even if I didn't
need another convert, I'd still want her to come. To meet Shep,
to know the truth.*

To be with me.

Jeff crossed his ankles on the footrest, linking his fingers
behind his neck. *The flowers just might convince her.*

It hadn't helped any, he was certain, that Alyee managed to get three of her giggly friends to come to the
concert with her the previous Saturday night.

Jeff had been miserable, trying to peel Alyee off his arm
all night so he could do his work. Shep, evidently very
pleased, had greeted each girl with the warmth he gave only

to the prettiest. They seemed to get caught by the music, swaying, clapping, and singing with the group when asked.

Jeff had taken Alyee home first, in spite of her big pout. When he drove up to her house, he let her out of the car, but refused to walk her to the door. She flounced off with her hips switching like a horse's tail. Jeff raised his eyebrows and bumped his head getting into the car. The girls inside giggled, and home they went.

Around school, Jeff heard the whispered gossip of his wild date with Alyee. Deanna couldn't help but hear about it.

Mrs. Sanchez used a mouth harp to encourage her Spanish class to stand. "It's time for the pledge, students," her crackly voice announced. The entire class mumbled the pledge in Spanish, with hands casually placed somewhere on the body. With the pledge over, Mrs. Sanchez hummed on the mouth harp again, and the class moaned through "God Bless America," again, in Spanish.

Jeff focused his attention on the Spanish work. The other kids in the class were there to make it through school. Jeff was there because Shep wanted him to be, because the greatest members of the Flock knew at least two languages beside their own. How else could they get the best jobs, the jobs with the government, in the embassies, with tour groups, and so on. Math to keep the books, languages to rule the world. Nothing else mattered.

* * *

Deanna didn't know what to make of Jeff. Five minutes with him, and she thought there was something there that could make a difference in her life. But then, he had his girlfriend. She shook her head over her history assignment. Why would he talk with her when he was clearly heavily involved with Alyee?

She forced her mind to focus on the history, but Jeff still hung out in the corner of her mind. At one moment a kind, gentle guy, and at the next, a two-timing leech. *He's got to be one or the other, or else he's schizo.*

The brown sky hung over the quad like a drape in a smoker's house. Deanna stood, her arms full of white carnations. "Where did you get all those?" Kathy asked her, waving her solo flower.

"I don't know," Deanna said with an embarrassed smile. "They all say: FROM YOUR SECRET FRIEND. I've gotten two in every class."

"Do you recognize the handwriting?" Linda asked as she broke the stem on hers, and tucked the flower in her thick black hair.

"They're all typed."

"Well, what a mystery," Kathy said. She turned and winked at Linda, who snuffed out a laugh.

"What are you two grinning about?" Deanna asked.

"We just think it's cute that you got so many flowers from some unknown person," Kathy said.

"Or persons," Linda added.

"Or persons," Kathy quickly agreed.

"Did you two send these?" Deanna asked, disappointment flagging her voice.

"Oh, no!" they chorused honestly.

Deanna frowned, not knowing whether to believe them or not.

Linda turned to Kathy to twist the conversation into a pleasant bow. "Who is your flower from, Kathy?"

"Didn't I tell you? It's from Dan!"

"Dan Roberts?" Deanna asked.

"Yes. I went out with him on Friday night."

"Must be serious."

"Serious fun," Kathy said.

Deanna laughed at Kathy's animated face and wild gestures as she described the evening. "Can I talk to you a minute?" a whispering voice startled her.

She spun around to see Jeff looking quite hopeful. He

raised one eyebrow and one side of his mouth into a questioning smile.

Kathy froze, mid-sentence, and said to Linda, "Hey, I forgot something in the library. Will you help me look for it?"

"Of course," Linda replied, ignoring Deanna's pleading look for them to stay.

"Yes?" Deanna said, looking impatiently at Jeff.

Jeff looked around, and Deanna rolled her eyes at his obviously sneaky attitude. "I've got to talk fast," Jeff said, looking into her eyes. "Every time I stand still, Alyee comes and attaches herself on me. Look, I know things look bad to you. . . ."

Deanna raised an eyebrow and smirked. "*Bad* can hardly describe it."

Jeff looked at the ground a moment, then again in her eyes. "I'm sorry. I want the chance to explain. But I know I'll never get the chance here. Can I meet you at Pepe's after school?"

"I don't want to sneak around behind your girlfriend's back."

It was Jeff's turn to roll his eyes. He groaned. "I knew it! I knew somehow this whole thing would get all twisted. Okay. If you won't meet me, is there any harm in my calling?"

Deanna thought a minute, her eyes scanning the crowds. "I guess not. As long as you don't lie to Alyee about it."

"Hah!" Jeff said with glee. "I would love to tell her about it and tell her every word of our conversation. But I'm too nice for that. What's your number?"

Deanna gave it to him, and he scratched it on his Pee Chee folder mixing it in with a million other scribbled phone and page numbers, notes, and doodles. A genuine smile crossed her whole face. "Aren't you afraid you'll lose it?"

Jeff became aware of the mess on his Pee Chee. He

smiled with her. "No, I'm not worried. I don't forget the important things." He glanced up and noticed a group of girls headed for him. "It's time for me to exit," he said hastily, and scurried off toward the rest room.

* * *

Deanna raced home along the residential route. She hated to admit it, but she was anxious for Jeff's call. After dropping her wilting carnations into a cut-glass vase, she pulled the telephone into her bedroom and stared at it between homework questions. The moment it rang, she pounced on it. She slammed the receiver on the wrong number, mumbling to herself about the idiots who don't even know how to dial a phone.

It rang again, almost immediately. She scowled at the phone, trying to decide if it was worth answering to tell the jerk to call someone else for a change. After seven rings, she decided he wasn't going to give up, so she picked up the phone. "Hello," she said in her most irritated tone.

"Oh, hi. I was just about to hang up. I thought you weren't home."

"Jeff!"

"Well, at least you sound happy to hear from me."

Deanna pulled her lips together in a wrinkled cushion. "Surprised," she said truthfully.

"Listen, Deanna. I asked to meet you at lunch two and a half weeks ago because I saw you carrying a Bible."

"Yeah," she said softly.

"I was impressed, because I'm a Bible student too."

"You are? You sure don't act like one."

Jeff sighed. "I'm sorry it looks that way."

"What do you mean *looks* that way? Don't you think your behavior is a little out of context with the Bible?" Deanna pulled the phone closer to her bed, then flopped on the pink spread.

"I think Alyee's behavior is making it look like mine is

out of context with the Bible. You see, Deanna. She's not my girlfriend."

"She wouldn't say that."

"I know. She tells more stories than I've ever heard. The whole thing embarrasses me and I don't want to hurt her, so I keep quiet."

"The way she hangs on you . . ." Deanna protested.

"Have you ever tried getting rid of a determined boa constrictor?"

Deanna laughed. "Okay, I think I understand. But what about the concert?"

"What about it? I ask everyone at school to attend the concerts. I think they have good music and a good message that will help everyone. She is one of the people I invited a long time ago. She came once, and has been pestering me ever since to go again."

"Terrific. Maybe she's getting helped by the concerts."

Jeff snorted. "Hardly. She has male, warm body on her mind."

"My, aren't we conceited!"

Jeff sighed. "I didn't mean it that way. She hangs on every available guy at school. My open concert invitations looked like date material to her."

"She's cute. You'd think every guy in school would be after her." Deanna twisted the phone coils around her pencil.

"They are. But somehow, I'm the lucky one."

"You don't say lucky like you mean it."

"I don't. Hi, Mom! Oh, sorry, Deanna, Mom just walked in. Anyway, I thought you might like to go to one of the concerts with me. If you like it, you might want to come to one of our Bible studies with me on a Thursday night."

"So, I'm just another kid to invite for you to get brownie points?" Deanna asked without a hint of meanness.

Jeff cleared his throat. "No." His voice grew quiet.

"You're very different from the other girls at school. I'd like to get to know you. It also seems like you're looking for something. I watch you wandering around the quad, with your nose in the Bible, the moments spent gazing at the ceiling in class. I think the group I attend might have some of the answers you're looking for."

Deanna hesitated, astounded. "Are you psychic or something? How did you know that about me?"

Jeff swallowed hard, then he laughed.

"What's so funny?" Deanna demanded.

"I can't give out my secrets."

"All right, Jeff. Spit it out. The truth, or no concert."

"You really want the truth? You promise you won't get mad?"

Deanna rolled over on her back, staring at the ugly canopy. "I won't promise you anything."

"Okay. I'll tell if you promise to go to the concert just once, even if you're furious with me."

Deanna sighed. "It's a deal."

"I noticed you looked lonely. It was also obvious you weren't scouting the quad for available males. Then your Bible. I thought maybe you were in training to be a Quaker or something."

Deanna gave one loud "Hah!"

"So, I asked your buddy Kathy about you."

"Well, that little sneak . . . ."

"Hey, I tortured her until she talked. Don't be too hard on her."

Deanna shook her head, and rolled over. "You gave me the flowers, didn't you?"

"Well . . . ."

"I thought good Bible thumpers don't lie."

"Yes, I did."

Deanna paused, trying to think of something clever. An embarrassed "Thanks" was the only thing that managed to slip out.

"I hope you liked them."

"It made me, uh, feel kind of special."

"Perhaps you are."

Deanna pulled her pillow over her head in embarrassment.

"Are you still there?" Jeff asked.

"Yeah, I'm still here," came the muffled answer.

"Will you talk to me at school?"

"Hmm," Deanna came out from under the pillow. "If I say no, do I get the same torture as Kathy?" she teased.

"Perhaps. The concert is a week from Saturday. I'll pick you up at seven if I don't talk to you before then."

"If I have to."

"You promised."

"Bye, Jeff. Thanks for explaining things. I'm glad you aren't such a creep."

"Me, too. Bye! *Wait!*" Jeff called into the phone.

Deanna lifted the receiver back to her ear. "What?"

"You have to tell me where you live."

"If you're so psychic, you can guess." She hung up the phone, hearing shouts of protest on the other end. She smiled, knowing she had her insurance he would call again.

=4=

The next week and a half flew in an awkward haze of shy looks, phone calls, and lunches under the tree. Deanna didn't care anymore that Alyee came by with her friends every day to swoon over Jeff. She thought it rather hysterical, knowing how Jeff felt. She could see his discomfort, and wished she could reach over and squeeze his hand. Somehow, she knew that would only embarrass him even more.

One hot day, after three sets of girls came over, one group popping up as soon as another left, Deanna said to Jeff, "You sure are popular. I wish I was that popular."

Jeff blushed. "I'm not really. It's just that . . . that . . ." he stuttered.

"That you're the best-looking guy in school."

The color on his face deepened. "That's not what I meant." He scooped up his things and left. Deanna felt terrible and apologized the next day in a note she dropped on his desk in trig.

*   *   *

Deanna stepped out of the black Camaro. She looked around the crowded parking lot. Gold patches of light near the ground pocked the night. Muffled sounds of shouting and laughter bubbled out of the windows and the narrow stairwell. "Jeff, you didn't tell me it was in a basement."

"Does it matter?" he asked, concerned.

"I guess not. I just . . . I'm nervous, Jeff."

"Don't be. This is my family."

Deanna's brows furrowed in confusion, her freckles disappearing into the cracks.

Jeff noticed the look and waved a hand at her. "Don't try to understand now. You'll understand later."

Deanna held onto the cold steel handrail as she walked hesitantly down the stairs. Jeff bounded down ahead of her and yanked on the heavy brown door, the oblong window fogged over from the inside.

The echoes of two hundred voices pressed fear and shyness into every part of Deanna's body. She felt very aware of each move, each step into the room. Her heart beat thickly and she felt it all the way inside her ears. *God, I'm scared*, she whispered in a tiny prayer.

The kids seemed to be walking on springs as they bounced from one person to another. A series of long tables with alternating pink, purple, and white paper tablecloths lined the back wall. Fresh-faced girls with bright pink cheeks and shiny round eyes stood behind, fluttering about, pouring punch, and pushing doughnuts.

At the opposite end of the room, tangles of clean-cut, fashionably dressed guys—maybe college age—were setting up sound equipment on a makeshift stage. In one corner of the stage sat a man, surrounded by many of the kids. A pale blue shirt hung loosely over his sturdy form. His hair, like Jeff's, danced about his head in oak-colored curls. His broad smile and happy laughter calmed Deanna's heart just a bit. Jeff followed her gaze and said, "That's Shep, the Shepherd. Our leader. He is a real man of God."

"He's a real something," Deanna replied reverently. "Look at his face."

Jeff smiled, his face showing the comfort and contentment of one who knows. "I look at it all the time. I can't seem to keep my eyes off his face. And his words. Oh, Deanna. Wait till you hear him speak. You'll know what he says is right."

"Jeff!" a bright voice called from behind them. Deanna felt her insides shrink a little when she saw a terribly cute blonde approaching.

Jeff opened his arms to her, and her petite body melted into his bear hug. "Debbie! I haven't seen you in so long."

"I've been involved in mission training, and it has been recommended I stay away for a while."

"Terrific!" Jeff exclaimed, giving her another bear hug. Deanna thought she should just fade into the wall.

Debbie smiled at Deanna and held out both her hands and took Deanna's. "Jeff," she said, still smiling at Deanna. "You've brought a friend. I'm so glad. What's your name?"

Deanna opened her mouth but nothing came out.

"Her name's Deanna. And she's a special one. I know God called her to be part of the Flock."

Deanna cocked her head in confusion and looked at Jeff. "The Flock?"

Debbie squeezed Deanna's hands, then let them fall to her sides. "The Flock, the Family, whatever you want to call it! The place where God speaks and God lives. The place where everyone finds what they are looking for!"

Instead of being comforted by such positive joy, Deanna felt something inside her urge her to leave . . . run . . . fly . . . anything—*just get out.* She swallowed hard and chided herself. *Deanna, you know I told you that you've got to get rid of that stupid shy part of you. This is only a test. There's nothing wrong here. Just a bunch of kids who love God. Since when is that wrong?*

Deanna stopped staring at her feet and tried to smile at the teeming multitude of kids surrounding Jeff to say hello. Everyone who could, got a hug, both guys and girls. It made Deanna feel funny to see Jeff hug a guy. She didn't know of any guys who hugged other guys . . . except . . . . *Oh, Deanna, you're so gross.*

The stage came to life all at once, with a resounding drum roll. Jeff grabbed Deanna's hand for the first time ever, and led her through the crowd, up to the front, and they sat on the floor with the rest of the group.

Deanna wished Jeff hadn't let go of her hand as soon as they sat down. She didn't feel quite as safe or protected without it. When the music started, she no longer felt so out of place. The music—contemporary, but not hard rock—was fun. Whenever she listened to the words, they touched her heart in a strange and compelling way.

> If you haven't got a home, or your home
> Cannot hear, cannot see
>   that you are there,
> Come to the Flock, Come to the Flock.

> If you haven't a person who will love you for who
>   you are,
> Instead of for what you do, then
> Come to the Shepherd, come to the Shepherd
> For he will love you.

Silly songs followed fast songs. Peaceful songs followed love songs. They swayed, they clapped, they stood up and cheered. One song called for stamping and clapping and shouting, "Hallelujah!" Deanna would have felt stupid if she didn't join in. Besides, it was kind of fun.

During the whole concert, Shep sat in his overstuffed

chair at the corner of the stage, smiling, clapping in rhythm, shouting encouragement between songs. Deanna looked at him and thought she could feel his dynamic presence. She liked him and wished she could get to know him. Out of the corner of her eye, she could see Jeff, with a soft smile on his face, absorbed in Shep's presence.

By the end of the evening, Deanna felt less shy. She could actually smile at the other kids and talk to them about school. Their talk seemed slightly childish, coupled with their round eyes full of wonder and excitement. After a half hour of socializing with doughnuts and punch, she could pick out who was a visitor, like herself, and who belonged. The difference was very distinct, yet she couldn't quite put her finger on why that was so.

It bothered her a bit that there was a continued sameness about them. Talking to Debbie was the same as talking to Janelle, who was the same as talking to David or Charlie. She hadn't noticed it at first. It took a while to realize she was saying the same things over and over. The same answers to the same questions. She shoved her silly thoughts and questions to the back of her head and shamed herself for being so critical of such nice people.

In an instant, silence surrounded her, except for one voice. A mellow, soothing voice. She could have been in the midst of a circle of whispering trees. She looked toward the voice, and saw Shep approaching her group. The group turned as one toward his voice, their faces reflecting the peace in his.

She noticed they all reached out to touch the hem of his shirt. His brown eyes made contact with hers, a depth to them that held her gaze. He stopped in front of her and took her hand. As he stroked it with his large, strong hands, he smiled. "A new, little one," he said in his mellow voice. "What is your name?"

Deanna could hardly whisper. "Deanna Clark."

"Well, Deanna Clark. I can see in your eyes you want to follow Jesus."

"Yes, sir."

"How much do you want to follow Jesus, Deanna Clark?"

"With all my heart, sir."

"I am the Shepherd of Jesus' Lambs, Deanna. You don't have to call me *sir*. I love the Lambs of Jesus, and I know their names. I won't forget yours, Deanna Clark."

Deanna gulped and nodded. He gave her a soft, gentle hug and flowed away from the group. Deanna turned and stared after him as the group began chittering excitedly. Several came and touched Deanna, as the group broke up.

As she and Jeff rolled out of the parking lot in the Camaro, he looked at her shyly. "What did you think?"

Deanna shook her head to toss away the dreamlike state she felt herself in. She was about to say something about Shep, and then stopped. It was almost as though if she did, it would pop something inside. So instead, she said, "Everyone is sure friendly."

Jeff sat up straighter and looked down the street before turning onto it. "Now can you see why I call them family? They are the only brothers and sisters I've ever had."

"Are you an only child?"

"Didn't I tell you?"

Deanna shook her head. "I guess you just take for granted that everyone has more than one kid in the family."

"Not mine. I've always been very lonely. You must have brothers and sisters then."

"Just sisters. Three older ones. I think I was an afterthought or something. I'm four years behind the youngest one."

"That doesn't make you an afterthought."

"Mom says they liked the first three so well, they decided to have one more to round out the numbers." Deanna looked out the window and locked the door. "I think they were hoping for a boy. But they'd never tell me that."

"Hmm," Jeff agreed. "I often feel like an afterthought even though I know I was the most planned-for baby in this state, if not the whole country."

"Why do you feel like an afterthought then?" Deanna rolled down the window, sticking her hand out into the rushing air. It felt good, after the stale air in the basement.

"My folks are too busy in their own little worlds to care too much. They are so glad I belong to the Flock because Shep keeps me in line. Shep does all the work, and my parents get all the glory," Jeff said bitterly.

"So how'd you find Shep?"

Jeff slowed to a stop in front of a Bob's Big Boy. "I know you probably aren't hungry, but I could use a Coke as an excuse to talk some more."

"Okay. My parents have no curfew. My sisters were such wonderful kids, they don't see any reason to put one on me. I've got all night." She rolled up the window, and shoved the door open. Popping down the lock, she closed the door. "Nice car."

"It's my mom's. It's a little too fancy for me."

Deanna felt her jaw drop. "A car that's too fancy? Come, on, Jeff."

"I mean it. In the Flock, we don't need fancy or unnecessary things. All I need is transportation. I've asked my mom if I could just have an old VW Bug or something. But she insists I take this." Jeff waved his hand over the shiny hood. "It's got everything a guy could die for—CD player, radio, mags, real leather interior. And I don't care. It seems a waste."

Deanna opened her mouth to comment, and shut it again. She grabbed his arm. "Come on, I'm thirsty."

They sat in a corner booth, as far from the rest of the

people as they could get. Deanna ordered iced tea and asked again, "How'd you find Shep?"

"Actually, I fell into the Flock. I was going to Parkside Presbyterian Church, and Shep was hired to be the youth director. There were about thirty kids in the group. In one year that exploded into over one hundred and fifty."

"Wow!" Deanna exclaimed.

"After the group hit three hundred, Shep felt he would be able to reach more kids if he left the church and went to some place where kids would not feel threatened by the church building."

"So he chose a basement."

"He didn't have a whole lot to choose from. All the other places large enough to hold his groups were only rental halls. He didn't have enough money to build his own, so he found a sympathetic businessman who owned a large office building with an unused basement gym."

"That explains the hardwood floors."

"And the basketball hoops."

"I didn't notice those."

"We camouflage well." Jeff leaned back and stretched his arms over his head. He smiled.

Deanna wiped the dripping glass. "Tell me more about Shep."

Jeff shook his head slowly, his smile fading as he considered an answer. "I'm really not supposed to talk about Shep. We are to focus on talking about the True Word, our relationship to the others in the Flock, or how to reach the unsaved. Shep does not like us to talk about him."

"Why?"

Jeff leaned forward over the table. He looked about to be certain no one was listening to their conversation. His voice dropped to a whisper. "I'm not a True Lamb yet, so I shouldn't really answer that. But one reason is that he does not feel worthy of any talk. Nor does he want false rumors to get about. Only True Lambs are supposed to reveal the truths about the Flock and Shep."

Deanna looked around too, feeling awkward again. "I don't understand."

Jeff pulled a napkin from the metal dispenser and wiped the circle of water from underneath his Coke glass. "Before you become a True Lamb at eighteen or older, you are part of the Flock, but you don't have the extensive teachings that the True Lambs have had."

"That's dumb."

Jeff looked up at an elderly couple, waiting for them to pass before he continued. "I used to think so too. But then I realized it's like getting college level math in elementary school. When you are eighteen, then you are emotionally and mentally better prepared for learning deeper things."

"Hmm," she thought out loud, stabbing at the crushed ice with her straw. "I suppose that makes sense."

Jeff's face lit up, his eyes dancing. "Wait till you hear him talk about the Bible. You know the man is in touch with God. He makes it all so alive and interesting."

"He's got me sold, then," Deanna said, hoping Jeff would believe her, even though she didn't mean it. With true sincerity, she added, "I try so hard to understand the Bible, but sometimes it just doesn't make sense."

"It will if you listen closely to Shep." Jeff reached across the table and gently touched her hand. His eyes searched hers. "Deanna, the Lord leads people to our Flock for a special reason. It means they were meant to do Work for the kingdom."

"What kingdom?" She wanted to ask question after question, if only he wouldn't move his hand away.

"The kingdom talked about in the Bible, the one that will be established here on earth."

"Oh, yeah. I was reading about that the other day." She paused, biting her bottom lip. "Do you really think that

God might have led me to the Flock, and that there would be something special for me to do?"

Jeff grinned so wide, Deanna could see the rubber band stretched from brace to brace in the back of his mouth. "Deanna, I don't doubt it. God leads Lambs like me to those He wants to choose—like you. I was aware of you from the first day you were at school. God never led me to Alyee or any of the others. Just you. That means you must be very special to Him." He gave her hand a tiny squeeze, then lifted his Coke to his lips.

Deanna watched his face, his concern for her. The sparkle in his eyes, the intensity of his words showed in his whole being. At that moment she knew she was totally and madly in love with him. She wanted to jump over the table and hug him.

Jeff slid his empty glass out of the way. His voice lowered. "I am also positive God has chosen you because of your math ability."

"Math? What does that have to do with anything?"

"Shep says that math and languages are the most important gifts for a True Lamb to have. The other studies are worthless because they can't promote the kingdom."

Deanna thought her heart would burst with joy. She'd shove all her doubts in the garbage disposal just to believe God had chosen her out of a couple thousand kids at Central High for a special purpose. It probably wasn't true, but who cares? It was something to believe in. And something else to have the best-looking guy in school believe God was using him to bring *her* to the Flock. She'd go for it! What did she have to lose? She could play Jeff's game until she could get him away from the Flock.

Then again, the Flock concerts are kind of fun. There's no harm in going where Jeff feels the most comfortable. Deanna smiled at Jeff. "This is the most wonderful thing that's ever happened to me."

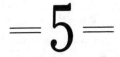

=5=

="S o, Deanna," her father asked, twirling his fork in a mass of spaghetti, "what was this Flock meeting like?"

"I'm not sure how to explain it. Kind of like youth group—and kind of not."

"You could start by telling me how many kids were there," he suggested.

"Oh, I don't know—lots. It seemed like the place was filled with kids."

"That could be ten or two thousand depending on the size of the place." He took a hunk of French bread, turning it red by sopping up the globs of sauce on his plate.

Her mother reached over and patted Deanna's arm. "You know your father likes exact numbers, Deanna."

Deanna placed her fork down on top of the coiled pasta. She furrowed her brow and dabbed her napkin on a spot of sauce that dripped onto the blue place mat. "What do you want me to do—count?"

"Estimate, Deanna. Can't you make an approximate estimate?"

"I don't know—two hundred? Two hundred and fifty? I heard somebody say that worldwide there are over a thousand young people involved, with more being added every day."

"A thousand, you say." Deanna's father raised an amused eyebrow in the direction of her mother. "What kind of building is it in?"

"It meets in a gymnasium. It's a little bit bigger than a basketball court, because they used to play basketball in there. It's got those neat wood floors, cement walls with a wide blue stripe going around the bottom."

Her father shoved his plate away, pushed back the chair and sighed heavily. "A place that size could easily seat three hundred. Are you sure it's not three hundred, Deanna?"

"Oh, Dad, how am I supposed to know? They have tables for punch and cookies set up in the back. They've built a kind of a stage at the front. We didn't sit in chairs. I guess so they can squeeze more kids in if they ever need to. Then they don't have to move chairs every time they change what they're doing."

Her father seemed to chew on his cheek a moment. Her mother watched him, and then turned her attention to clearing the table. "I'd like to see what it's like myself sometime, Deanna."

Deanna groaned. "Oh, Dad. Please don't. I'd *die*."

"We'll see."

All weekend Deanna thought about Monday and seeing Jeff again. Just the thought of his brown eyes and soft smile made her feel shy. Maybe it was because he thought something about her that no one else did—that God had chosen her, a little nobody, number four in a house of girls, to be a special worker in His kingdom. But it was probably more than that absurd thought. She'd never been in love before. She didn't know how to act or what to say. She did know she would do anything for him, be anything for him. She wouldn't even tell him how stupid he was being for believing God would choose her for something special. Nobody would choose her.

Could he tell she loved him? What if he could? What if he couldn't? The dilemma in her heart was making her crazy.

When she saw Jeff on Monday, he looked as shy and confused as she felt. He told her he had work to do at lunch, and couldn't be there under the tree. Then he scuttled away as if he were afraid. Deanna wondered if he was avoiding her.

Tuesday afternoon she volunteered at Children's Hospital, wishing the whole time Jeff was her checker partner instead of José. She put all her men in front of José's on purpose, so he would win. "Hey," José protested. "You're not tryin'."

"I'm sorry, José," she said, pushing the board away from her. "I guess I'm just thinking too hard about other things."

The smile dropped from José's little face. He pulled on the wheels of his small chair, and rode away down the hall. Deanna sighed.

Wednesday changed the frustration to joy. Jeff spent snack and lunch with her, smiled and wrote notes to her in English and trig. Every part of her felt warm and wonderful.

As the days and weeks passed, Deanna felt more and more as if she walked on air. When Jeff smiled, it was for her, and no one else. She had a look she could give him in return that caused him to drop his eyes, and blush just a little. She made him a batch of chocolate-chip cookies every Sunday and stuffed them into his locker on Monday.

They went to another concert together. Deanna hung back, while Jeff helped set up tables, speakers, mikes, and carry in Shep's chair. She couldn't keep her eyes off him the whole night. His presence could be enjoyed forever without tiring of it. When they stopped afterward at Bob's Big Boy, she realized she hadn't heard any of the concert.

"Deanna, wasn't that concert great?" Jeff asked, as he slid across the vinyl bench.

"Oh, yes," she lied. She wiped a splatter of some liquid off the seat with a napkin, before placing her purse there. "I can't wait for the next one."

"I was hoping you'd say that." Jeff leaned across the table, his smile melting her into the vinyl. He turned away to place their order, then turned back to wait her response.

"Why do you care if I enjoy the concert?"

"If you didn't enjoy the concert, then I couldn't invite you to a Flock meeting, now could I?"

Deanna felt her heart jump a tiny bit. She looked up at the waitress who set their drinks and fries before them without a word.

"Does that mean you're asking me to go?" she said quietly. Then picking up her usual carefree attitude, she said, "I thought you'd never ask."

Jeff dipped a French fry into the mound of catsup. "I, uh, was going to, but some other things came up."

Deanna cocked her head, and wrinkled her nose. "Lots of things are coming up, aren't they?" she said, half seriously.

Jeff looked at her, startled. "What do you mean?"

"Either you're awfully busy, or you're avoiding me," she said coyly, licking the catsup off her fry.

Jeff stared out the window at the cars zipping past. "I have been busy. It's hard to keep up with two languages, especially when you've got the pressure I have."

Deanna tried to look into his eyes to see whether she should believe him or not.

He chose a fry and offered it to her with a smile. "It's a peace offering. Forgive me?"

"Of course."

On Monday and Tuesday, she couldn't believe it. She could swear Jeff was avoiding her *again*. She cried through three miserable volunteer hours—little drippy tears that would pop out at the oddest times.

That evening, when her mom called her to the phone, she knew it had to be Linda calling for help on her trig.

"Hi, Deanna," Jeff said as if he'd spoken to her minutes before. "I promised to take you to a Flock meeting. Can I pick you up at seven on Thursday?"

"Do you really want to?"

"Of course, silly. See you then?"

"Yeah, sure."

*   *   *

The black Camaro drove up at seven sharp. Deanna bounced out of the house with her Bible under her arm. She yanked open the door, and slid into the bucket seat.

Jeff stared at her Bible. "Why'd you bring that?"

"Isn't this a Bible study?"

"Yes." Jeff pushed the stick into first gear. "But Shep does all the Bible reading."

"I thought I'd bring my Bible to read along," Deanna said as she pulled the shoulder strap down and buckled herself in.

"You really don't need to read along," Jeff said firmly.

Deanna thought he seemed nervous. "You don't want me to take my Bible in, do you?"

Jeff's throat moved in a gulp. "It's just that, well . . . no one takes a Bible, because it looks like we doubt the truth of what Shep is saying if we take our Bible. We are to trust Shep and that he knows the Bible better than any of us."

"Does he?"

Jeff stepped on the brake a little too hard to stop at the signal. "Of course, he does, Deanna. Have you been to seminary? Do you study the Bible and its intricacies with prayer all day long, every single day?"

"Don't get nasty, Jeff. I was only asking. Remember, I don't know anything about Shep."

Uncomfortable silence rode with them the rest of the way to the meeting.

The parking lot didn't look as full as the nights of the concerts. The excited voices of the students bounced around the basement. Again, they sat on the floor. Deanna leaned over to Jeff and whispered in his ear. "Couldn't they use chairs just once?"

"They're such a hassle to move around every time we change format. It never hurt anyone to sit on the floor."

"Anyone who had enough padding, that is," Deanna moaned, rubbing her tailbone.

"Just think of all the money we save by sitting on the floor," Jeff added. "We can learn just as easily without them."

"Speak for yourself. Hey, why doesn't Shep sit on the floor then?" Deanna teased.

Jeff sighed. "Deanna, we have to be able to see him. Besides, he deserves more than we do because he is a man of God."

Deanna stuck her lips out in a pout. "I think that's stupid. Besides, I was only teasing."

The sparkle left Jeff's eyes, and they turned to ice. "Then you can leave. This is a holy place where we learn holy things. I don't question what our Shepherd does, and neither does anyone else. If you want to hear the Bible in clear, practical terms, then listen. If you want to make a fuss or joke over little things, then sit in the back and you don't have to come next time."

Tears popped into her eyes. How dare he make her feel like a bad little girl! She was about to get up and go to the back, when Shep came in and sat in the chair. His magnetic presence held her still.

The voice of whispering trees floated out into the room. "Oh, Lord, our most High God, be with us and teach us tonight through Your undeserving servant. Amen."

Amens rippled through the room and all was quiet except for the rustling pages of the Shepherd's Bible. "Tonight, our message will be from John, chapter ten."

The ice in Jeff's eyes had melted, and the look of devotion Deanna wished was meant for her came over his face. She shifted her body so her knee would touch his, and lay her hand between them, hoping he'd pick it up.

A little screaming ball inside her told her how stupid Jeff was being to so adore this person they called Shep. How dumb to accept whatever he said without questioning. *But if he is God's messenger, I should listen, right? Mom says pastors are God's mouthpieces. He speaks through them. So I'd better listen. Maybe I'm the stupid one.*

Her thoughts tried to poke and prod her, but the demanding, kind voice of the Shepherd pulled her away from those thoughts. She listened to him read the Word of God, and explain it to the eager ones before him. He talked about the Flock, loving it, and laying down his life for it. How the Shepherd gives up all things to take care of the sheep.

His voice was one of complete authority. No hesitation. It demanded obedience, but the demand was kind and not unreasonable. She forgot Jeff sitting beside her, forgot the others in the room, and could only hear the voice of the Shepherd.

Shep would recite, his Bible open on his lap. He glanced at the page, as if for reference, then looked at the eager crowd to speak. "Even the Father knows me and I know the Father. I lay down my life for the sheep."

He poked his finger on the page and looked straight at her. Her face froze, her eyes riveted to his. "And I have other sheep which are not of this fold: I must bring them also and they shall hear my voice and they shall become one Flock with one Shepherd."

An exclamation point of fear and excitement popped into her heart at that moment. "Other sheep, which are not of this fold. . . ." Could that be her?

She could not look away from Shep, for his gaze still held hers. His voice wrapped her in a cocoon of love and purpose. "The other sheep are wandering aimlessly, not finding what they need where they are. We must find these sheep and bring them into our Flock . . . ."

Murmurs of approval hovered in the room.

". . . when they hear my voice, they will know the truth and the truth will set them free. Free to have peace. Free to have protection in the arms and fold of the Shepherd. And in the fold they will become True Lambs of the Shepherd, and he will give his life for them."

His eyes swept through the group, enticing them in. "And you, my little lambs. You have found the fold. Now go, help the Shepherd find the sheep who are not of this fold. Bring them in with love."

Shep had already left the stage when Deanna felt herself almost wake up from something—as if she had been in a trance. Like coming out of a dark theater after a gripping matinee, only to find life continued as normal outside. It took a few minutes of reorientation to distinguish the real from the fantasy. The only difference was the now and what had just happened, were *both* real.

Jeff popped up to his feet and started greeting those around him. Deanna couldn't join in the talk. She still felt too disoriented. Someone she remembered as Barbara encouraged her to come have cookies and punch at the table. Deanna followed along like a little puppy—or *lamb*.

A bright, bubbly girl with round eyes and flushed cheeks served punch. "Hi! I don't think I know you. You're Jeff's little friend, aren't you."

Deanna bristled at being called a "little friend," but

looking at the girl's face, realized she didn't mean anything negative by it. "Yes, I am."

The girl stuck her hand out, and Deanna shook it, feeling rather silly. "I'm Josie. I'm so glad you came tonight. Jeff has been sharing with us how much he thought of you."

"Oh, yeah?" Deanna said, feeling wonderful that Jeff would think about her even when she wasn't around. "My name is Deanna."

"Do you think you'll come back, Deanna?"

"If Jeff asks me."

"Well, if he can't bring you sometime, I'd love to."

"Thanks, but I don't know if that's really necessary."

"No, I'd love to do it." Josie handed out plastic cups of punch with a big grin between every couple words.

"Josie. Are you serving Deanna?" Jeff said, as he walked behind Deanna.

Deanna turned and smiled at him. Josie handed him an extra-full glass of punch. "Of course I'm serving her. Not only a glass of punch, but a gallon of love. That's my job. Oops. It's time to close up shop. Sharing time in two minutes."

Deanna looked up at Jeff. "Sharing time? I thought this was over."

"Are you kidding? We have at least another hour's worth."

"Oh," Deanna said, disappointed.

"Do you need to get home?" Jeff asked anxiously.

"No, not really. I just didn't realize this would be such a late night." Deanna moved out of the path of the kids beginning to move toward the stage.

"I'm usually home by ten-fifteen. Is that too late?" Jeff looked apprehensive, glancing at her, then at the stage. Deanna could tell the sharing stuff meant a lot to him. He didn't want to miss it.

"Okay," Deanna said without meaning it.

The group all moved without a command toward the stage. *Sheep to the pen*, Deanna thought rudely. She mentally slapped herself.

Her behind was sore from sitting on the hardwood floor for so long. *Everyone else must have calloused buns*, she thought with a quiet giggle.

Shep returned with a few blue aerograms in his hand. "All right!" Jeff exclaimed. "Letters from the missionaries."

"Missionaries?" Deanna asked.

"Shh. Listen."

Shep paced the stage, opening the top letter. "Dear Family," it began. "Life as a missionary is all I ever hoped it would be. The people love to hear about Jesus and God's Word. They come to our meetings, and many have become sheep. Our Shepherd's cassette tapes are vital to this work. Perhaps soon, we will be able to have our 'one Flock with one Shepherd.' Adios, familia."

The next two letters sounded surprisingly similar, although one came from France and the other from Japan. That didn't seem to bother anyone but her. It did make Deanna feel good to think that this tiny group had missionaries, and people were coming to God through them.

Sharing time lasted a very long time, with Lambs standing and sharing who they were trying to bring, how they were doing in their subjects, and how their families responded to their involvement in the Flock. Little claps followed each one, fingers tapped lightly on palms of hands. *Lotion claps*, Deanna thought. *As if everyone had a cushion of lotion making the claps muffled.*

Jeff stood and pulled Deanna up with him. "This is who I have asked you to pray for. Deanna has come, and has the potential for being one of the best Lambs we have. She excels in math, and is one of only two juniors in the senior trig class." Little pitter-pats of approval rained around them. Deanna ducked her head and sat quickly.

As Jeff promised, they were home by ten-fifteen. Deanna stood at her door, her face raised to look at Jeff. He backed away a couple steps. "I'm so glad you came, Deanna. I'll see you at school tomorrow?"

Deanna's expectant face fell. "Of course," she said flatly.

Jeff bounded down the steps and left Deanna, standing on her porch, watching after him.

May 16

The mothers got together in a darkened room. They had parked their cars in various places about the streets, walking stealthily through the shadows to meet in the house. The curtains were drawn, all the lights off. Newspapers, one, two and three days old littered the front walk. Junk mail jammed the mailbox.

It was rumored that Shep had spies everywhere—spies that didn't hesitate to use any method necessary to halt a meeting such as this one. Dissident parents reported being followed, changes in tonal quality of their phones—as if tapped. Even, some said, vandalism of their homes. No money was ever taken. Only papers, letters, and notes about Shep. If even one of these women had been followed, it would be trouble for the rest of them.

They entered the house alone, and with a key. No one said anything until they were all there.

They introduced themselves stating first name only, the first name of their daughter and where she had gone. Only one mother was not worried enough to come.

"Debbie worked so hard to learn Spanish. But it was easier than the math."

"My Sarah had to learn Japanese. She spent so many hours crying over it. But she denied that she cried."

"How many letters have you written?"

"Fifteen, at least."

"I have written twenty-five."

"I have lost count."

"To what address did you send them?"

"This one." A piece of paper was passed around the room. The women peered at it with only the street lamp outside to aid their vision. Each one nodded. The ones whose daughters went to Japan looked confused.

"We have not had problems with letters."

"You haven't?" the others chorused.

"What problems have you had?" asked Sarah's mother.

"The letters are all returned, 'addressee unknown.' "

"Or, 'no such address.' "

A letter crackled as it was opened and flattened. "I'll read you my letter: 'Dear Family, Life as a missionary is all I ever hoped it would be. The people love to hear about Jesus and God's Word. They come to our meetings, and many have become sheep. Our Shepherd's cassette tapes are vital to this work. Perhaps soon, we will be able to have our one Flock with one Shepherd.' "

"Oh, no!" a woman cried out. "That's the same letter I received from my daughter."

The snap of a purse was heard, rustling noises, and a sniffle. "May I have a tissue too, please?" asked the neighbor.

"Me too."

"And me?"

The small packet was passed around, and each mother removed a tissue for her own needs.

"Who else has received this letter?" a voice of authority spoke out.

A count was taken. All had. Typewritten, no return address.

"When did your daughter leave?"

"March sixteenth."

"Mine too."

"And mine."

"All left on the same day."

"How do you know?"

The husky voice said slowly. "I was there. I saw them."

A uniformed gasp lifted the hunched forms.

"But no family was allowed."

"How did you get past the guards?"

The husky voice cleared, then spoke. "I dressed as an old woman. I took a suitcase and an old ticket folder. I hung back. I only saw those leaving for South America."

"Did your daughters have passports?"

All heads nodded in unison.

"Was the Shepherd there?"

"Yes. He hugged them all, lifted their chins, and kissed their foreheads. They forced smiles, wrapped their arms around each others' waists, and went on board."

"Did you follow Shep?"

"He hung around watching until the plane left. He turned to a hatted man who sat in a leather chair. He smiled and gave a thumbs up sign. He patted his wallet pocket and left. The man with the hat put his newspaper down, picked up his briefcase, and walked in the opposite direction."

A heavy sob shook the room. In the shadows, an arm could be seen rising, then lowering on the shoulder of the crying woman.

The voice of authority spoke again. "We've got to do something about this."

"But what?"

"We must talk with the Shepherd."

=6=

The Flock meeting ended early. "For the first time in a year," Jeff declared. He drove into Bob's parking lot.

"We'll be able to say, 'I'll have the regular,' pretty soon," Deanna teased.

The waitress smiled her recognition and took their order without writing it down.

Deanna drew on her napkin with a pen a previous customer had left behind. Her brows hunched together in deep concentration. Her bottom lip pressed against her top lip. Jeff reached over and lightly touched her arm. "What's wrong, Deanna? Something Shep said?"

"No," she said, her teeth grinding together.

"Then what is it?"

"We've been going to Flock and concerts for a long time, Jeff."

"Three months this coming Saturday," he said with a wide grin.

She laid the pen down precisely on the napkin. She looked around, to be certain no one listened. She lowered her voice to a whisper. "Are you gay?" she asked, her eyes searching his.

Jeff's face took on an expression of deep shock and sorrow. "No. Why do you ask?"

"Well, you never touch me, or kiss me, or try to . . . to . . . ."

Jeff's body sagged. "Oh, Deanna. It's only because I respect you as a creation of God. I see you as holy and special."

Deanna forgot to keep her voice quiet. "Why can't you see me as a little less holy? You're driving me crazy." The man seated behind her turned his head to look at the young couple and smiled.

Jeff grabbed the pen, clicking the cap off and on. "Deanna," he said, his voice so low Deanna had to strain to hear him. "Part of my life as a Lamb means that I must remain pure. I must not kiss you, or touch you, beyond a friendly hug once in a while."

"I don't even get a hug, but the other 'precious Lambs' get one," she said with a teary frown.

Jeff put his hands in his lap while the waitress put the fries, Coke, and iced tea in front of them. "Thank you."

He stared at his hands until the waitress left. "If I hugged you, Deanna, I couldn't stop. Sometimes I hide out in the library or in Cramer's classroom with the excuse of tutoring failing kids, just to stay away from you. I have to until I can get my thoughts under control again."

Big tears rolled out of Deanna's eyes and landed in splotches on her napkin. "It just doesn't seem fair, Jeff, that I finally find someone I can really love and care about, and I can't even give him the affection I'm dying to give."

The man behind them got up to leave. He helped his wife from her seat, and both smiled at the young couple as they passed. Jeff ignored them.

"Deanna. I wish I could do what other guys do. Sometimes it kills me not to. But you see, my whole life is . . . is given to Jesus."

"Then why don't you take it back," Deanna demanded throwing her napkin on the table.

Jeff stared at his hands a moment. Then he looked up at her with great kindness. "I could if I wanted to. But I really don't want to. My life has purpose. There is always someone there to talk to when I need them. Someone who hears what I say. Not someone who listens only during radio commercials or between phone calls, or from behind a newspaper. And there's peace inside, and sometimes there's love, and joy, patience for irritating people and situations. Something wonderful's going on inside me, and I don't want to lose it."

Deanna licked her salty fingers, then wiped the grease on her napkin. "Do you think a few kisses will make you lose it?"

"You are a Christian—you've accepted Jesus as your Savior, haven't you? I thought you'd understand," Jeff said in a strained, pleading voice.

"There's not many people who will take me as I am, Jeff. I'm too quiet, too smart in a difficult subject, and I have zero confidence. I like Jesus because He doesn't have any high or 'must be beautiful' standards. He likes me anyway." Deanna shrugged her shoulders and took a sip of tea. "I'll follow anyone who'll think I'm okay. I guess I don't see Jesus in the same way you do. I don't think He gives a rip whether I kiss someone I love or not. And I can't see the point in giving Him every minute of my life. I don't think He cares that much."

Jeff put the last fry in his mouth. He reached for the bill, accepted Deanna's offer of a dollar, and slid out of the booth. "Let's go?"

Deanna nodded. *Maybe I should just shut up and go along with what he says,* she thought as they walked side by side to the car.

*   *   *

Deanna volunteered to work every afternoon at Children's Hospital the next week. The kids were thrilled to see her day after day. And day after day, Deanna saw Jeff in everything that moved. She saw him when a mother hugged her child. She saw him when the intern praised her, his smile revealing a mouthful of braces, one rubber band in the back. She saw him in every smiling face.

She would give anything to be with him every minute. Anything.

On Thursday afternoon, General Supply handed her a stack of boxes to take back to the floor. Her rubber-soled shoes made soft flumping noises as she walked through the hall. Her vision turned inward. She saw herself with her arm looped through Jeff's. She pictured herself on the darkened front porch, her chin lifting up, his eyes closing as he kissed her.

Depositing the boxes at the nurses' station, she decided she would turn him around. She would make herself so irresistible that he would take her in his arms as though he would never let her go. A chill went up her spine.

"Miss Clark," a little voice pierced her thoughts as a plump hand tugged on her dress. "Miss Clark, will you please read me *Quick as a Cricket*"?

"Okay." She read from memory, not paying attention. She put the child and the book down, and went into the Volunteer Office to resign.

At school on Friday, Deanna decided to play social butterfly. She smiled at everyone, with a discerning eye out for Jeff.

"You have been so depressed this past week, Deanna," Kathy remarked at snack. "What happened to pull you out?"

"Oh? I don't know. Just decided to get out, I guess."

She gave Jeff her best smile across the quad, and continued to talk with Kathy and Linda. She laughed with them, fingering the note she would leave in Jeff's trig book next period. Her mind only heard part of what they said.

The days flew by and Deanna hardly noticed the heat wave sweltering southern California. She wrote notes to Jeff three times a day—one for trig, one for English, and one for his locker. She kept the conversation happy and full of laughter whenever Jeff called.

At the end of May, the hottest day on record melted even the most stalwart heat lovers. Deanna looked all over school, all morning for Jeff. At lunch, she stood on one foot, then the other, juggling her change in her hand. Both phones were occupied by jerks who thought they owned them. "C'mon, be polite," she finally whined. One of the callers quickly hung up and hurried away.

She dug a piece of worn paper from her wallet. She dropped the money in, punched the buttons, and waited. After the twelfth ring, Jeff answered. "Hi, Jeff, is something wrong?"

"Deanna," his sleepy voice answered. "I'm so sick. I can hardly move. My joints hurt so bad. And to top it off, I have a dumb fever."

"In this heat?"

Jeff groaned. "Don't remind me."

"I'll bring you something cool after school."

"You don't have to do that," Jeff said unconvincingly. "Don't you have a standard thing with Linda to help her with trig?"

"Yes, but who's more important? I'll see you after school. Bye!" She hung up quickly so he wouldn't have a chance to talk her out of it.

She found Linda and Kathy hovering near the cafeteria exit. "You guys waiting for something?" she called.

"Oh, sure," Kathy said. "We're waiting for someone to bring us some leftover yummy food from the cafeteria."

"Hey, Linda, I have some bad news," Deanna said.

"You don't look like it's bad news."

"I have to cancel our afternoon tutoring session. I've got an errand I have to run."

Linda's chin started to quiver. "But Deanna," she said in a soft, pleading voice. "Tomorrow is the last pretest before the final. I've got to do well on it. And I don't understand chapter fifteen at all."

"I'm sorry," Deanna said, trying to sound disappointed. "But this errand must be done. I really have to do it."

Linda turned her head away. Kathy tapped her on the shoulder. "I'll try and help, Linda."

Linda sighed, her face tight with trying to hold back the tears. "You don't understand it any more than I do."

"Maybe if you called Jeff, he could help you," Kathy volunteered.

"He's sick," Deanna said a little too quickly.

They both looked at her, and Linda nodded. "Oh, I understand."

Kathy nudged her. "Let's go, Linda. I'm sure we can find someone who cares." She shot Deanna a nasty look over her shoulder, as they disappeared into the crowds. Deanna shrugged her shoulders and skipped up the stairs to her locker.

Jeff's house was nestled in the hills above the college. People had to have more than a little money to live there. Deanna trudged up the steep hill backwards, sweat dripping down her back. She wondered if the ice cream would make it in the heat.

She rang the doorbell twice and knocked three times before the lock snapped and the door opened. Jeff's hair stuck out all over his head, his face pale and drawn. He clutched a maroon terry robe around his middle. "Come in," he said.

He walked hunched over, an old man without a cane. He dropped on the sofa spread with a sheet. He curled up into a little ball, closing a blue Lamb Guidance book. He struggled to give her a smile. "Hi."

"Jeff, you look awful."

"I feel worse. Count on it." He closed his eyes, and pulled the robe under his chin.

Deanna stood above him. "I brought you some ice cream." Jeff didn't respond. She wiped her sweaty neck underneath her sticky hair with the back of her hand. "Do you want some now or shall I put it in the freezer?"

Jeff stayed still. Suddenly, he said, "Huh? Oh, put it in the freezer. I think I'll have some in a few minutes, okay?"

"Okay." Deanna walked through the spotless rooms to the kitchen. The stainless steel refrigerator/freezer was the largest she had ever seen in a home. She added the carton of ice cream, and popsicles to the full freezer.

She unconsciously tiptoed back to where Jeff rested. She sat in a Queen Anne chair and watched him shiver and twitch. Moving to the couch, she perched on the edge next to Jeff. Her hand hovered over him, then came down on his arm. She stroked it softly, then took his hand in hers. She kissed it lightly. It was like a switch had been thrown inside her. She stroked his arm some more, and then kissed his cheek. He turned his head toward her, his arms reaching up to pull her close. She kissed him long and hard.

He suddenly stopped and let go of her. "I think I'll have my ice cream now," he said politely.

Deanna smiled. "I'll be happy to get it for you . . . sweetie."

Deanna hated herself for acting like Alyee. But now she knew why Alyee did it. To get affection from Jeff, you had to take it.

*   *   *

The Flock meeting seemed different without Jeff. Deanna sat with Josie, who corralled her the minute she walked through the door. "I'm so glad you came on your own, Deanna!" she squealed. "It's too bad our little Jeff is sick."

Before Deanna could cringe from the syrupy tone, Josie

gripped her elbow and steered her to the center of the room. "Look, everyone, Deanna's back!"

Lambs surrounded her, bleating their hellos, and touching her as though she were a rare commodity. Deanna wished she hadn't come.

The singing and Shep's voice soothed her. His harsh words of the Vinedresser lopping off unfruitful vines and burning them came across as words of love. For here she was, a part of the vine. She was only a baby shoot, not yet expected to bear fruit. Pictures filled her mind of tiny tendrils and baby leaves making her drift. . . .

"An announcement!" A voice seemed to shout in her ear. She sat up straight, her eyes popping open. Josie giggled and squirmed next to her.

"Summer camp is coming in just five weeks. All Lambs need to come to the quiet place of the Shepherd to hear his words, admonitions, and directions. It will last two weeks, and the cost is cheap. I have pamphlets here for everyone, and a special one to give to a friend."

Josie leaned over, her head almost in Deanna's lap. "Oh, you will come, won't you, Deanna?"

Deanna's eyebrows raised as she looked at the beaming face beneath hers. "Uh, I don't know, Josie. I think that's the same week as our church camp."

"Come to this. I bet your camp is only one week, and ours is two. Please come."

On the way home, Deanna thought it over. *Two weeks with these loonies?*

They aren't loonies. They are special people, chosen out of the world to serve God in a special way.

Now you sound like them.

Wouldn't it be nice to be someone special? Chosen by God Himself?

Whoopee.

Jeff will be there.

I'll go.

66

=7=

="W"hy don't you want to go to our church camp, Dee?"

Soapsuds flew into the air as Deanna dipped the skillet into the filled sink. "I like the kids at Flock better, Mom. Besides it's two weeks' long, instead of just one."

"Then it's twice as much," her father said. "Thank you, dear," he said to his wife, dipping a spoon into a mound of chocolate-covered ice cream.

"No, Dad, it's not. It's only ten dollars more."

"How can they feasibly do that?" he wondered out loud.

Deanna sighed. "I think it's because they own the camp, Dad. Everyone takes turns cooking and cleaning up and stuff, so they don't have to hire other people to do it."

"Hmm. You complain about doing the dishes here. Are you going to complain there?" he asked between bites.

"Dad," she whined. "It's different there."

"I think we should let her go, Bob."

He let his spoon fall onto the plate beneath his ice-cream bowl with a clatter. "Well, it looks like I'm overruled."

"It's not like that, Bob. Now stop it."

"All right, Alice. Deanna. If Deanna washes the pans every night for two weeks, until the money is due—without complaining—she can go."

Deanna raced over to her father, hands dripping soapsuds. "Thanks, Dad!" she said, kissing his cheek. He only grunted in response.

"I've got to call Jim, Alice. We've got another major problem to unscramble."

Deanna's mother sighed. "Can't they ever take care of things themselves?"

"It's my job, Alice." Deanna's father stood, then left the room, his eyes dark with concentration.

Mrs. Clark picked up his empty dish, rinsed it, and put it in the dishwasher.

"Dad gripes at me because I complain about cleaning pans, and he can't even lift an ice-cream bowl from the table," Deanna muttered.

"Hmm. It's the way of men, Deanna. You'd better get used to it."

"Shep's not like that. I bet he'd be the one to wash the pans."

"What do you think of this . . . Shep, Deanna? What's he like?" Mrs. Clark picked up a towel and began to dry the skillet.

"I don't really know, Mom." Deanna paused, then scratched her nose, leaving a white stack of bubbles on the end of it. She wiped it on her shoulder. "I guess the best thing I can say is that he knows the Bible better than the youth director at church. He cares about every single one of us, and knows us by our names. Mr. Simons doesn't ever get my name right."

She plunged her hands back into the water, searching carefully for the sharp knives. "When Shep talks to us

68

from the Bible, I can really see in my mind what he is saying. He never says, 'I don't know,' like Mr. Simons does. He cares, he really cares about each of us."

"And Jeff has a lot to do with your going too, doesn't he?"

Deanna blushed. "Of course, Mom."

"And that's the biggest reason you want to go to that camp." Her mother looked at her expectantly, her head tilted to one side, just like Deanna did when she listened to her friends.

Deanna scrunched her mouth and looked around for another pan. "Of course not," she lied.

"Of course so," her mom replied with a smile. "Why do you think I prodded Dad so much? We want you to have fun and learn more about the Bible. You seem to think you learn more when this Shepherd guy talks about the Bible. And you most certainly will have more fun if you are with Jeff . . . ."

Deanna threw her arms around her mother.

*   *   *

Deanna tried to pretend the phone didn't work all weekend. She paced the floor wishing Jeff would call. She played tennis with Kathy and Linda, after helping Linda with trig for two hours to make up for Thursday afternoon. Once at the court, she wished she wasn't. She couldn't concentrate on tennis when only four blocks away stood Jeff's house. Three times she missed the ball because she was looking up the street, hoping that maybe Jeff would be out for a walk.

"That's a set!" Kathy called.

"I love a good workout," Linda said, slipping the headband from her glistening brow.

Deanna jammed her racquet into her bag. As she pulled out a towel, a handful of camp brochures fell out. "Oh, Kathy, Linda, I forgot to give you one of these. It's for camp. I thought it would be fun if we all went."

Kathy took one look and groaned. "Oh, no. Not *this* one."

"What's wrong with it?" Deanna demanded.

Kathy shook her head. "They're weird, Deanna. You don't want to go spend two weeks with those whackos."

"No kidding," Linda agreed. "I went to a concert with Jeff once . . . never again."

"I go all the time," Deanna pouted. "I don't see anything wrong with it."

"That's because you're going to be with Jeff," Kathy said.

"So they're a little strange. What's wrong with that? You think Jeff is a nice guy—and he's one of them."

"Yeah," Linda said hesitantly. "But there is a difference with Jeff."

"He may be there, and be a part of them," Kathy added, "but he isn't one of them."

"He sure would disagree with you," Deanna said.

"I know he would. But time will tell. You watch. He won't be with them forever. He'll wise up one day."

"I doubt that." Deanna put the brochures back in the bag and zipped it. "Jeff is totally sold on being a Christian."

"Being a Christian is different from being a part of a group," Linda said.

"But it's a nice group," Deanna defended. "The leader teaches the Bible, and really knows his stuff."

Kathy picked up a stray ball, batting it over the fence to the players in the next court. "Maybe so, Deanna. But something fishy's going on there."

"Like what, Kathy?" Deanna dabbed the towel on the back of her neck.

"Like I don't know what. But like I said, I went there, and I knew something was wrong. Mr. Simons warned us about going there after we came back. He thinks it's a cult or something."

Deanna put her arm through the straps, throwing the gear bag over her shoulder. "I think Mr. Simons is jealous. In his wildest dreams, he could never come up with more than thirty kids. Until I see anything wrong with the Flock, I'm still going."

Linda zipped her bag. "Be careful, Deanna. Stick with Jeff and don't let them brainwash you."

Deanna tipped her head back and laughed. "Brainwash? Are you nuts? A nice group of kids, a man who teaches the Bible, how much more harmless can you get?"

"Just be careful," Kathy said again.

Linda reached over and placed her hand on Deanna's arm. "And don't forget we'll always be your friends."

"Don't be dumb," Deanna said. "Come on. We've got to get back to work on that trig. Only two weeks until finals."

*   *   *

Jeff returned to school on Monday, still pale, still moving slowly. In English, he bent over his book, afraid to see Deanna arrive. Afraid she might hate him.

Deanna blew in with the tardy bell. She snatched up the note resting on her desk. "I'm sorry," it said. "I hope you will forgive me. I was wrong to let my desires get out of hand. May we still have lunch?"

I loved your out-of-hand desires, Jeff Bradley. You may let them get out of hand anytime.

Lunch came too soon for Jeff. From a distance he watched Deanna settle herself onto the bench. He gulped twice, put on a smile and strode over to the bench. Without a word, he pulled a small wrapped package from his backpack, and set it on her lap.

"What's this for?"

"Your birthday."

"You're a week early."

"I know. I wanted to also say how sorry I am."

Deanna looked into his eyes. "You're no more sorry than I am."

Jeff turned his head away. "Deanna, don't," he whispered.

"Okay, okay." She unfastened each end with care, wanting to save the paper for her scrapbook, where Jeff's notes were pasted. The box rattled as she turned it over. She lifted the black lid. Resting on a cloud of cotton, glinting in the sunshine, was a floating heart on a serpentine chain. "Oh, Jeff," she breathed. She lifted it and fastened it around her neck.

Jeff cleared his throat and studied his thumbs. "I got it to let you know you are always in my heart, but to remind you that Jesus is there first." He paused and looked at her. "I hope your feelings aren't hurt."

Deanna wiped her eyes and kissed him on the cheek. "I'll try to remember who you are, Jeff Bradley, and to respect that."

She put her face in her hands and cried softly. Jeff put his arm over her shoulders, and she leaned her head against him. "I'm sorry I act like such an idiot," she said, as she dug through her purse for a tissue. "I'm just so afraid I'll lose you."

Jeff squeezed her shoulder, then let his arm fall. "You won't lose me. There's nothing wrong with being second in someone's life, Deanna. And that's the highest place anyone will ever have in mine."

Deanna blew her nose. "I guess I'm so used to being last in someone's life that I figure it's either first or not at all."

*   *   *

Jeff took large strides to gain more of the hill in a smaller amount of time. He turned up the stairs to his house. "Mom, I'm home!" he called, as he opened the door.

"I'm on the phone, Jeff," she called back.

Jeff walked through the hall and dumped his khaki pack

on his bed. As he took off his shoes, his ears picked up the phone conversation drifting down the hall.

"Of course not . . . Jeff would never do that . . . You ought to get Tommy into the Flock . . . sure I think it's great . . . No . . . Don't be silly. There's nothing spooky about it. I know because we've known Shep ever since he took over the youth department at Parkside several years ago. He's a nice man . . . Millie, it's great. You get Tommy involved and you never have to worry about him again . . . No, I really don't worry. Shep is the parent. It gets all the responsibility off my back. I never did like being a parent in the first place . . . No, Millie, I didn't say I don't like Jeff. I love Jeff. I only said I didn't like being a parent. . . ."

Jeff closed his door. For once he wished he had the stereo his dad had offered to get him. He would have turned on the hardest rock music as loud as he could.

*   *   *

The last three weeks of school blurred into late nights of study, finals, headaches, and heat. Linda passed trig—barely. Jeff and Deanna watched as Kathy and Linda accepted their diplomas in black-robed honor.

Deanna spent much of her time fingering the floating heart, and less time with friends, church, or family. She filled all her pockets of time with thoughts of Jeff, and wishes that things were different. She thought of hundreds of ways to change Jeff, but knew none would work. Her plan became to shower him with her love. She could not get enough of him, and could not wait for the day when he would feel the same about her.

She looked forward to camp when every waking moment could be spent with him.

*   *   *

Jeff reached for the phone. He knew Deanna's number by heart, but still, he stared at it. He had gone over what he would say, a hundred times in his mind. But none of those times did it sound right. How could he let Deanna go to camp without telling her that they wouldn't be together? The rules would not ever be bent, not even for a stubborn, smart girl like Deanna.

His stomach pulled together, sympathetic with his agony. He argued in all directions. That Deanna was better off not knowing. In the long run, they would be together. A True Lamb Deanna was far more touchable than a Deanna who lived and breathed outside the Flock.

Jeff hung his head in shame, over the silent phone. Not telling her was cruel. But would she go if she knew? Seeing Deanna even at a distance was better than not seeing her at all.

Jeff leaned his sweaty brow against the rough spread covering his bed. "Oh, Lord, what would You do?"

The voice of the Shepherd sprang to help. "Any method in bringing lambs to the Flock is pure and acceptable."

Jeff replaced the phone on the table, and began to pack.

=Deanna wiped the dust from her eyes, then licked her dirty lips. "Come on, sing, Deanna," Josie urged.

Deanna clapped her hands and tried to get the sound past her parched throat. *How do they sing for three hours straight, and continue singing after thirty minutes on a dusty road?* she wondered.

Josie shrieked, followed by a busload of "hallelujahs." Deanna stuck her head out the window and saw a hand-painted sign with an arrow pointing to the right. Scrolled green letters read GREEN PASTURES. *What a hokey name. It sounds like a cemetery.*

"Oh, Deanna," Josie bubbled. "We're almost there. Oh, I can't wait. It's just like Psalm Twenty-three. The still waters, the table before us, our cups overflowing. There's nothing like the Green Pastures where our Shepherd leads."

Deanna licked her lips again, her dry tongue hesitating

over the parched skin. She couldn't wait to see the still waters. Any waters would do.

The bus bumped to a stop. Clouds of dust swirled around it, eliciting coughs from the squealing campers. Deanna looked around at the flushed, excited faces, hands resting on cheeks, eyes wide with joy. *They look like a bunch of six-year-olds.*

Josie grabbed her hand, and dragged her down the emptying aisle. "Deanna, let's go quick. I want to see where the Shepherd will put us this time. He is so clever in choosing the right spot. Oh, I'm always so *happy* here. Each time I come, I wish I never had to go home. Two weeks is too short to spend in paradise. Just think, in no time, Christ's new kingdom will be established here on earth, and this will be the center of it."

Josie's words bopped around inside Deanna's head. Josie always talked too fast, too much, and too bossy. Deanna would have liked to tell her to shut up. But if tolerating Josie was the price she had to pay for two weeks with Jeff, she would gladly pay it.

She had reluctantly boarded the bus without Jeff. She thought it stupid to have separate boys' and girls' buses. But with the memory of Jane and Paul making out in the back of the bus the year before, she decided this group took the easy route to preventing similar incidents. Stupid, but tolerable.

She watched the boys' bus empty in the opposite direction, as all of them whooped and hollered up a hill to a small red building at the top. Josie dragged her to another building, a shabby green one, with the paint peeling in large, shiny pieces.

"I need a drink," she whispered to Josie.

"Not now," Josie pleaded. "We're going to get our cabin assignments. I don't want to miss it. Shep's helpers only give them once."

"You get the assignment, I'll get water."

"*No!*" Josie said sharply. Deanna thought she saw fear jump into her eyes at that moment. "You wait until we get our assignments." Her hand clamped tighter around Deanna's, as she yanked her inside the building.

Deanna sat on the splintery floor with the other girls, her hand still in Josie's grip. *How did I get myself into this mess? Jeff. It's always because of Jeff.*

Shep's helper, Carol, read off names and cabin numbers in her cheery voice. A squeal of delight met each announcement. *Sounds like a bunch of baby pigs.* Josie let go of Deanna's hand to clap along with her squeal. They would be in Mercy Cabin, wherever the heck that was.

"It's right between Forgiveness and Gift," Josie whispered, as if she could read Deanna's mind. "Ooooh, I told you it would be perfect."

*   *   *

Jeff walked backwards up the hill, trying to catch a glimpse of Deanna. He could not drum up the enthusiasm his "brothers" had. Perhaps it was the heat or the dirt. *It's Deanna.* Jeff shook his head. He wasn't supposed to think about girls other than as a sister. How could Deanna ever be a sister? She was more than that. He hoped she would always be more than that.

Samuel trotted up, spun Jeff around, and linked his arm in Jeff's. "C'mon, bro. You'll miss your cabin assignment. Don't worry about the sisters." Samuel laughed. "As a matter of fact, you'll be free of them for two whole weeks. Two weeks of pure Shepherd's love and words. Man, I can't think of anything better."

Jeff sagged. *It's going to be worse than I thought. The separation rule never bothered me before.*

There's never been a Deanna before.

Now Jeff felt terrible that he had encouraged Deanna to go to camp—with a twinkle in his eye he had hoped she wouldn't miss. Turmoil mushed up the insides of his stomach. He wondered how could he survive without talking to Deanna for two weeks.

Samuel started to run the final few yards to the "barn," dragging Jeff behind him.

*   *   *

"Isn't it perfect?" Josie cried. She shifted her duffel bag to the opposite hand and started up the short path to the cabin. Deanna stared at the lopsided building in front of her. The fourth stair of six had a warped board missing. The waist-high cabin walls gave the impression the builder hadn't thought privacy or weather protection necessary. A canvas roof rested on beams that stretched straight out like a spider's legs, then dropped down to the half walls. The centerpole looked as strong as a matchstick. The east-side canvas walls rolled up to the roof level, giving everyone a clear view into it.

Deanna followed Josie into the cabin. She first noticed twelve rolled mats stacked in the corner. "Our beds," Josie said proudly. Deanna glanced at the old floor, relieved to see it swept clean.

Twelve footlockers lined the opposite "wall." Each of the ten campers and two counselors chose a footlocker, and dropped her gear inside.

The counselors gathered the campers in a circle in the center of the floor. The first counselor turned to the second and in a sing-song voice said, "What's your name, and why are you here?"

The second counselor sang in response, "My name is Mary, and I serve the Shepherd." She turned to the girl next to her and sang, "What's your name, and why are you here?"

The girl responded, "My name is Elsa, and I want to become a True Lamb."

The song-talk continued through the group. The new girls stumbled over their names as well as the answers.

78

The ones who sang the same tune as the counselors won a cheerful "Good for you!" from them.

Deanna thought the whole thing was stupid, but didn't know what else to do except play the nonsense game halfway. In a low, quiet voice, she said, "My name is Deanna, and I came to spend two weeks at camp."

The counselors' faces turned to stone, and Deanna felt like crawling inside herself. She quickly turned to Josie and sang, "What is your name, and why are you here?" The counselors' faces changed to a look of utter happiness.

Josie's voice twittered like a bird as she announced, "My name is Josie, and I want to help our newest Lamb, Deanna, learn what a joy it is to love Jesus and follow the Shepherd."

A warm bubble burst over Deanna's head and showered her in a lovely feeling of someone caring about her, personally. She knew God supposedly cared about her this way, but here was a person, someone with skin on, someone who could be seen, who cared. It was like Jeff, all over again.

She wondered if Jeff was in his cabin, sitting in a circle, singing silly words and names and questions.

She closed her eyes and thought-prayed, *Jesus, help me to have a good time here these next two weeks. Help me to get used to the way they do things here. Because I know they love You, and that's the most important thing.*

"*Deanna!*" a sharp voice pierced her prayer. She looked into the eyes of the lead counselor. "What are you doing?" she demanded.

"I . . . uh . . . I was pray . . . ing, Sharon."

Sharon's face lost the edge of anger, but still bore signs of being annoyed. "I'm glad you feel free to pray anywhere, Deanna, but you must understand that the Bible says in Ecclesiastes that there is a time for every purpose under heaven. And the purpose now is to get to know each other. You may pray later. We even have a beautiful little chapel to use."

"I'm sorry," Deanna said softly.

"I'm sorry, will you forgive me?" Mary corrected.

"I'm sorry, will you forgive me?" Deanna restated.

"In the name of the blood of the perfect Lamb, I forgive you," Sharon said in a lofty tone. She sat straighter than before, a smug look across her face. If Deanna didn't feel like such a whipped child, she would have been tempted to slap her across the face.

Sharon began a list of "recommendations for the best possible week at Green Pastures." *They sound like a bunch of rules to me,* Deanna thought.

No smoking at any time, in any place. If you have any cigarettes, please either trash them or give them to the counselors. If they are found in your possession, you will be excused from the camp.

No drinking of alcohol at any time. Water and two kinds of soft drinks are all that are permitted.

Deanna's mind jumped and startled at the "recommendations." They tempted her to ponder in anger and confusion over some of them, until another absurdity caught her attention. The counselor spoke too fast for her to think too long on one subject.

There will be no communicating with the males in this camp by females, unless it is a male counselor with the purpose of interacting about the recommendations or the Truth about the Word of our Shepherd or total commitment to Jesus Christ.

Deanna's eyes grew wide, and filled with tears. *But I came to be with Jeff. Can't I even talk to him?*

Josie caught her hand, squeezed it and smiled at her. Deanna held back her urge to stick her tongue out at her. There wasn't much else she could do. *I've always made the best of things before; looks like I'll have to do it again.* She hadn't intended for her sigh to be heard by Sharon.

Sharon's sharp gaze pierced her through. "And if anyone has difficulty with the recommendations, they may be excused from camp, and from the presence of the Shepherd."

A few girls gasped, as if no worse fate could befall anyone, than to be cast from the Shepherd's presence.

At last, Deanna got her drink. She had to stick her head under the spigot at the watering trough which had been set up with eight spigots outside a group of cabins. Josie stood right next to her, smiling all the while.

As they wandered toward the meeting hall, Deanna could see why Green Pastures just might be a place where paradise could begin. The meadows, like great green pools, were held together with clumps of trees. Sometimes, Josie told her, you could find a very tiny meadow nestled in the midst of many trees.

Legend told that it was here, in one of the tiny, hidden meadows, that the Shepherd first heard Christ's call to lead His sheep. The Shepherd had been running from all the evil in the world, tired of fighting the Prince of Darkness. He came here to run away, when Christ stopped him, hedged him in the meadow with a blinding light, and told him that he had been chosen to lead the sheep.

The Shepherd had fallen on his face and proclaimed his unworthiness, Josie told her in a holy whisper. But Christ had told him that He had been looking the world over for a new Shepherd to lead His lost Lambs—the ones truly dedicated to Him. In the Shepherd, He found someone as tired of evil as God Himself—someone who had the strength and devotion to Christ necessary to keep the Lambs together in the flock.

Deanna nodded and listened to Josie's voice, softened and slowed by reverence. They stopped for a moment at one of the three brooks, listening to the gurgles as it splashed in its happy journey. "Even the brooks seem happier here," Josie whispered after a moment.

A breath of wind ruffled the trees, which seemed to agree in voice with Josie.

Josie turned upstream, and Deanna followed her to a large, stone building. Voices ringing with joyous song filled the air. "Uh-oh, we're late," Josie said as she picked up her step. "We usually meet ouside during the daytime, and in here at night," she explained over her shoulder.

As they stepped inside, Deanna lifted her chin and scanned the audience. There. No, over there, sat Jeff. His body swayed with the others to the beat of the song. All at once, Deanna noticed that the chairs on the left side of the center aisle were filled with male bodies. All those on the right side were filled with female. "It's so we can have more fun with the competition songs," Josie giggled, again as if she could read Deanna's mind.

They slipped into the third from the last row. Deanna would have been very happy to be in the last row, but since every seat up closer was full, and the last two rows empty, she assumed they followed another "recommendation" and kept her mouth shut.

Jeff couldn't keep his mind on the singing. He wanted so much to look over to the other side of the aisle, and find Deanna. He wanted to wave and smile at her, to somehow let her know he hadn't brought her here to drop her. The fourth time Samuel's elbow jabbed him, Jeff gave up his wandering thoughts of Deanna. He pasted on a phony smile, and gave what looked like his whole self into singing.

As the singing continued, Deanna felt herself losing the anxiety over the recommendations. The sneaking suspicion that something was very wrong began to melt away. How could people who love Jesus so much, and sing to Him so sweetly be wrong? *I must be wrong.*

She jumped up and down with the others during the competition songs, singing as loud as her strained voice would carry. She collapsed into giggles after they sped the song up so much they all got confused and were jumping up and down all over the place.

Her body swayed through the slow songs, her hands lifted high during the singing of Psalm 23, the theme song at Green Pastures.

The hard metal of the folding chair disappeared as Shep began to talk. His words of love, of acceptance, pulled her like a magnet, until she felt clutched to his chest. She closed her eyes to listen to his words, and started when Josie flicked her—*hard*—with her finger. "We listen with our eyes on Shep," Josie explained in a tiny whisper.

Deanna groaned to herself in frustration. *Next they'll be telling me when I can go to the bathroom and when I can't.* Shep's words swept away the frustration, and again Deanna felt his love and acceptance.

An hour passed, and Deanna fought tears that tried to fill her eyes. She no longer felt worthy of Shep's love and acceptance. Something in his words, in his phrases, made her see her own unworthiness. In her mind, she begged Jesus to forgive her, to find her worthy.

Soon, she gave up the battle with the tears, and they slid down her face. Totally caught by Shep, she did not hear the sniffles around her, nor see the tears on everyone's faces.

Another hour passed before she began to see how she could become worthy. No, not really become worthy, because that would never be possible. But she could study hard, she could be the best Lamb she could. She could memorize Scripture, bring others into the Flock. Oh, there was so much she could do, to show her appreciation for the Shepherd's loving her, in spite of her unworthiness. Into the third hour, her tears had dried. The group rose as one, singing *Hallelujah* to the Lord, and thanking Jesus for loving them enough to send a kind, loving Shepherd to care for them.

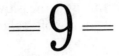

At dinner, Reb, the Shepherd's right-hand man, gleefully popped off the following day's activities. Deanna leaned over to whisper to Josie. "Do we ever get free time?"

"What's free time?" Josie whispered back with a smile.

Deanna couldn't tell if Josie was teasing or serious. *The Lambs never tease.* "You know, time to yourself to do what you want."

"Why would we need free time?" Josie paused a minute to bend her ear toward Reb, then let out a squeal of glee when he mentioned volleyball. "Our time is the Lord's. The Shepherd knows how much sleep a Lamb needs. He knows how much play a Lamb needs. How much teaching and food. He knows what is best."

Deanna was about to respond in a less than polite manner, when a cold, hard stare from Sharon stopped her.

Another meeting, then her cabin gathered for a time to respond to Shep's talk. Deanna sat, sullen, as far away from the rest as she could. There was no way she was going to let on that Shep's talk touched her deeply. She wasn't about to give anyone—least of all, Sharon—any thoughts that she might be cracking. *Because I'm not. I'm not obeying their rules on the inside, even if I'm forced to obey them on the outside.*

"Deanna," Sharon crooned, as if to a newborn, "How did Shep touch your life?"

"With his finger," she said, not expecting the choked laughter from some of the newcomers.

Sharon's face turned purple, her eyes bulging. *"You,"* she said, just under a shout, "can stand in a corner."

Deanna's eyes narrowed. "And what if I don't?"

"You will be on report to the Shepherd, and he will deal with you in his own manner."

Deanna examined this prospect quickly and thought the better of her defiance. She could play games with Sharon's authority, but she didn't dare test Shep's patience. She still was not about to stand in the corner for anyone. "Will you please forgive me for my rude behavior?" She dropped her eyes so Sharon wouldn't see the fire still alive in them. "I am known to become silly in my weariness. Here it is seen as defiance. I am truly sorry."

Sharon nodded her head. "Your sin is forgiven. But you must try to deny your past behavior, and take on the new behavior, the robes of righteousness from your Savior."

Deanna nodded, her head still down. She tasted blood from her lower lip, as she bit hard to keep from laughing.

Deanna gratefully crawled into bed at midnight. Unable to sleep more than an hour at a time on the hard floor, she finally sat up in the darkness. She slipped out of her sleeping bag and tiptoed among the snoring bodies to get out into the cool night air. She stopped at the top of the stairs to put on her tennis shoes.

She walked without fear, trying to step as an Indian—a trick she learned at church camp years ago. Over the bridge, and to the left. She wanted so much to know where Jeff was, and what he was doing.

Stupid, stupid rules. You can't leave the meetings for any reason, including personal ones. You can't call home. You can't receive any mail until the final day. And worst of all, I can't talk to Jeff. How can I possibly see him from a distance for two weeks? Not talk? Not touch? Not ask questions?

Leaving was a consideration. But it was too late to go to her camp. She'd stifle at home too. Maybe, just maybe she could find something fun here. Maybe she could find some sneaky way to see Jeff. This was only the first day. And they did plan some fun things. She might as well stay. It had already been paid for. *Now I'm thinking like my father.*

She stopped behind a tree on the west side of the dusty road the buses had traveled. She heard some talking. Poking her head around the tree, she saw three young men in military greens, one with a rifle slung over his shoulder. Their clean-cut faces shone in the moonlight. Hardened faces. Faces with a job to do.

Beyond them, she noticed the large gate the buses had trundled through only a few hours before. One of the young men pointed his flashlight toward the gate. A heavy chain with three padlocks hung through the sections.

The flashlight beam moved slowly over the gate, then beyond, into some bushes. "Anyone tries to get in or out of here has to deal with me first," the rifle bearer hissed.

The other two chuckled. "Ain't nobody gonna mess with you, Samuel."

Deanna gulped, terrified they would see her. She pressed her back against the tree, tiny splinters of redwood piercing her fingertips. In a moment, the redwood oil would start to sting her fingers. Her heart raced as the guards thudded by her on the other side of the tree.

Samuel said good-bye to the others and leaned on the opposite side of the tree Deanna tried to make herself part of. She tried to breathe with her mouth open—deep, slow breaths. Samuel began to hum some of the camp theme songs. Then he prayed that he would always be true to the Shepherd, and thanked God for calling him to become a True Lamb.

His harsh voice sounded superior to any of the other young "lambs" she had heard.

It seemed like a snail had gone to China and back before Samuel left his spot, and took off to roam again. Deanna left as quietly as she could, which also meant she had to go slowly. She could only whisper prayers that Samuel would not see her.

She slipped gratefully into her sleeping bag and fell immediately into a terrified sleep where evil, black lambs chased her with guns and sticks.

* * *

"Get up!" she heard Josie chirp, somewhere inside a cave. Sleep reluctantly left her as Josie tugged and pushed her sleeping bag about. "Come on, Deanna."

"What time is it?" Deanna muttered.

"A beautiful six-thirty."

"Oh, Josie, do I have to? I'll be up before breakfast. Summer is for sleeping in."

"Not at Green Pastures. We have to be out in ten minutes for Kangaroo Time."

"What's that?"

"Exercises. All good Lambs need their exercise."

"It's too *early*," Deanna protested. "Besides, I don't want to exercise."

"The Shepherd knows what his Lambs need. Let's go!" Josie reached down and took Deanna's hand, pulling her up from the floor.

"All right, Sister Lambs," Mary sang out. "Let's wash our faces and get to Kangaroo Time! We must support the K-Time leader."

Deanna noticed something strange. She couldn't figure

it out until she had rolled her bag and mat, and had set them at the side of the room. *No one groaned at Mary's announcement. Everyone gave whoops of joy instead. At church camp, everyone groans if they have to be at breakfast by eight. And that's without exercises.*

All campers lined up at the sink for a quick face and teeth wash, with only a moment to run a comb through the hair, and a quick stop at the outhouse before trotting to the main field.

The girls lined up on one side of the field, facing the guys on the other. Each did the same exercises, trying to outdo the other half. After each exercise, everyone bounced and cheered, clapping their hands.

Deanna felt the whole thing too dumb for words. But whenever she tried to sit out an exercise, or do it half-heartedly, she was poked from all directions until she picked it up again.

Jeff put all his energy into the exercises. He loved the morning workout. He watched Deanna across the way whenever he could. He tried not to laugh watching her attempt to sit out some of the hard work and fail. He got angry when the girls around her poked her until she started up again. He had never thought before what the exercises would be like for someone who wasn't interested.

He tried waving at her during the jumping jacks, hoping no one would notice such a horrible breach of etiquette. *She must not be able to see me*, he thought, disappointed.

A light breakfast followed the exhausting exercises. Then they were herded back to the higher meadow for a meeting.

*　　*　　*

The rest of the day didn't go much better than the morning for Deanna. Whenever she tried to do something a little different from the rest, someone was there to poke her, flick her, or frown at her until she did it right. When she did it right, she got showers of praise and smiles.

The meetings were long, playing with every emotion she had, and revealing some she had no names for. Shep's words mesmerized her. She felt lost, as if in the middle of a sea, drowning, until Shep lifted her into the safety of his boat that soothed, protected, and taught.

On the path to dinner, Josie held her hand and swung it. Deanna hated such affection, but had begun to not notice it as much anymore. She was not allowed to go to the bathroom by herself; Josie always went with her, chatting the whole way. Deanna noticed all the new girls had someone "attached" to them. It made her feel a little better to know she wasn't the only one.

Wherever Deanna went, girls she didn't know would pat her on the back, or touch her cheek, and say, "We love you."

"You are a precious friend."

"There is a place for you in the kingdom."

Deanna started feeling good inside. She forgot the fear and confusion that the guards and locked gate had put into her. All of that faded away like a bad dream. Instead, the emptiness, the gaping holes in her, were filled to overflowing.

Then a thought or a glimpse of Jeff would send her back to the frustration that churned inside. To be close to him, to touch him, to talk to him. Her mind wandered, as Josie stopped to chat with a friend.

Gentle words jolted her back to where she really was. "You must be special to God for Him to choose you to come to camp."

Her head reeled with the new thoughts Shep poured into her, the loving concern from all these strangers around her. She wanted time to think and sort out these new ideas, but she never had a chance.

After dinner, on the way to the meeting, she saw Jeff. Her heart fluttered. "Jeff, hi, Jeff!" she said excitedly.

Josie yanked on her arm as she suddenly remembered the rule about not even talking to the guys. She knew Jeff wanted to talk to her. She saw the smile on his face as he looked down to the ground, as if he hadn't heard. She was glad he hadn't forgotten about her.

Immediately Reb was at Jeff's side. "Why, Jeff, I thought you knew better. Shep says this is two weeks out from the pressures of life to focus on Him. You cannot serve two masters, Jeff."

Another counselor ran up to his other side. "Are you sure you are ready to be a True Lamb?"

Deanna shook her head, and tears of shame fell down her reddened face.

The counselor's words slapped Jeff. A True Lamb. Yes. He wanted to be a True Lamb—more than anything else in the world. To serve the Shepherd to the utmost of his ability. To be as close to God as anyone could ever be, was his highest goal.

A few days without Deanna couldn't hurt. They would have so much to talk about when camp ended. So much more they could share if they didn't spend so much time thinking about each other.

I will focus my thoughts and energies where they belong, Jeff decided.

Jeff looked at the counselor. "Forgive me for behavior unbecoming of a True Lamb."

Reb put a heavy hand on his shoulder. "You are forgiven, little one." The other counselor nodded his approval.

*   *   *

Each day, Deanna felt a little more like she belonged, and surprised herself by enjoying the structure of the day. While at first she rebelled at being denied the freedom of making her own decisions, she now enjoyed the greater freedom of not needing to think for herself. There was no failure when there were no choices.

The approval of the group began to mean a lot. It felt much better to have them smile, and pat her on the back, than to have them frown and turn away. Deanna found herself watching the others around her, to mimic them, to gain approval.

Somehow it mattered what they thought. If doing what they liked made them all happy, what was the harm in doing it?

Two hours out of every day was spent working. Some groups scraped paint off cabins, preparing to repaint them the next week. Some groups—only guys—dug into the mountainside, loosening rocks, uprooting trees, creating a path to somewhere. Deanna watched from her knees as she yanked out rotten floor boards and replaced them.

She and Josie worked alongside Karen and Sue, under the watchful eye of Sharon. The work was tedious in the hot cabins. They sang songs, and Josie and Karen quoted Scripture to help pass the time.

Fifteen minutes before quitting time on Thursday, Sue began to complain of thirst. Sweat rolled off her nose and chin, spotting the floor.

"Keep working," Sharon barked. "Only fifteen more minutes."

"Can't I just get a quick drink?" Sue asked, her voice weak and raspy.

"It is not time for water. It is time for work."

Deanna felt her head swimming with the heat. Her brain didn't seem to focus properly on the nail before her. She missed time and again, her blows becoming slower and further apart.

As she raised her hammer, she paused to wipe a drop of sweat from her eye. A loud THUMP was followed by a scream of anguish. She looked up to see Sue passed out on the floor, her finger split open and bleeding.

Quickly, she looked at Sharon. Her face had turned to stone. She shook her head and turned to walk away. Deanna rushed to Sue's side, holding her head, and talking to her. She eyed the purplish blob that bled profusely.

When Sharon returned with Reb, Deanna, Josie, and Karen were told to leave.

Josie yanked on Deanna's hand, pulling her away. "She needs to see a doctor," Deanna said.

"She needs to see the Shepherd. There are no needs the Shepherd can't supply."

"But, Josie, I could see the bone. She really hit it hard."

Josie looked angry. She threw Deanna's hand back at her. "You don't have faith, do you? One week at camp, and you still don't have faith in the Shepherd. His healing touch is all that girl needs."

"Sue needs a doctor. She needs the care of . . . ."

"She only needs the Shepherd. The sooner you learn that, the happier you will be." Josie marched ahead, crunching rocks and sending up dust clouds beneath her feet. She came to a bend in the path, and stopped at a small pine tree. She grabbed it in her hand, and swung around. "One word of this to anyone, and you will be sent home."

"What?"

"Because Sue didn't have enough faith, she got hurt. If she continues to lack faith, nothing anyone can do will help her. But your talking about it will only cause others to turn from the truth."

Deanna stopped several feet from Josie. "I don't understand."

"Don't try. Just listen to the Shepherd and shut out everything else."

By the beginning of the second week, Deanna had a funny feeling in her head. She couldn't think very clearly and felt like something was slipping away. She found herself shaking her head to try to make the pieces rattle into place.

Each time she asked questions about Sue's finger, she was told the Shepherd had placed his healing touch upon it. But Sue still wore an expression of pain, and covered it with what looked like a dirty rag. Josie wouldn't let Deanna near her.

Soon she forgot about Sue. To think about Sue would require her to think on her own, and that was not permitted.

Her body ached from not enough sleep and sitting for hours in the grass listening to Shep. Yet the fatigue from not enough sleep became natural, normal. The ache of hunger from not having quite enough to eat had disappeared. Through the exhaustion, her former questions about the group seemed absurd. Her heart soared from being full and content for the first time in her life. She fell into step with the others. She accepted all she heard without question.

"Deanna, your words are wise!" exclaimed those in her cabin group.

"How pleasant to have someone as wise as you," Sharon observed on Wednesday.

Deanna found herself verbally applauding others too. "How pleasant to see your smile in the morning, Carol."

Her face ached from continuous smiling. She thought less about Jeff, but still found herself looking for him when the campers did things together.

Friday night, a volunteer crew set up a stage outside by the campfire. Each cabin group had spent the final week of camp preparing for their time on stage. A song, a skit, a pooling of talent. Everyone participated.

Deanna sat in childish glee, immersed in each production. She swayed with the others to the music, clapped her blistered hands and laughed at the skits. Mercy Cabin put on a skit acting out the "Day in the Life of a Lamb." The group roared at the antics of those on stage. Shep sat in his corner, one hand over his mouth, his eyes sparkling and watching Sharon—the one who portrayed him.

At the end of the skit, he nodded his approval while the crowd applauded.

When the program had finished, a somber air swept through the crowd. They bowed their heads in humble anticipation, prayerfully awaiting this night of prophecy, of dedication. Each one who chose to, found a stick to toss into the fire with words of dedication spoken aloud to the group. Then, they would pass by Shep. If his hand lifted a tiny bit from its resting place on his robed lap, the person would stop, and Shep would prophesy over him.

The guys filed by first. Deanna hugged her knees to her chin, anxious, excited, extremely aware of every part of her surroundings. A breath of air touched her face and played with her hair; the grass, cold and prickly beneath her. The fire crackled with each tiny addition, blowing wafts of smoke in her direction.

Ten sticks were thrown in the fire. Ten pairs of sneakered feet paused in front of Shep's chair, and moved on without comment.

Reb stopped in front of Shep, and knelt, his head bowed. Shep stood and placed a hand on Reb's head. As he spoke, all of Deanna's awareness focused on the two in front. Everything else disappeared.

"Reb. True Lamb. A ram of strength, with horns curled and ready for battle. With wisdom you use those horns. With kindness you guide the sheep. You will be elevated to great heights in the name of the Father. Your work will be over the Lambs in this Flock when the Shepherd is called away."

The seated Flock let out a tiny *oh* sprinkled with gasps. The Shepherd had anointed someone to be almost as great as he. Reb would be listened to with new ears, ones ready to respect.

Many more lambs passed the chair, some with prophecies, some not. Jeff walked, as always, in humility, not even pausing by Shep's chair. Shep had to reach out to touch Jeff's arm. Jeff stopped. Reversed two steps. Knelt. Bowed his head. The Shepherd's hand rested on his head. Deanna held her breath.

"My little Lamb. The one committed as no other. To you, God has promised a royal place in His kingdom. You will be crowned as True Lamb when the time is ripe. Then your training, your work will begin. Unto us, the work of your thoughts will be committed. The old flesh will rot away, the reborn flesh will come. A high and mighty place you will occupy. Yet it will not be revealed what you shall be until the crown of the True Lamb is upon you."

Deanna saw his knees quiver as he stood, and was helped to the side by a counselor.

She didn't see or hear the rest of the prophesies. Pride for Jeff and a sense of awe consumed her attention.

Her group stood, Josie pulling her up. Deanna walked with stiff legs to the edge of the fire pit. She stared at the flames until she felt a shove from behind.

She threw her stick in, took a deep breath and said, "I, Deanna Clark, want to give my whole self to this family. To serve God in the best way I know how, as the Shepherd leads me." She felt a tremor pass through her. Because of fear or solidity of commitment she did not know.

What are you doing? the old voice demanded.

The faces closest to the fire glowed in tones of orange and yellow. They flickered from seriousness to smiles with her words.

She padded by Shep, and to her surprise, saw his hand lift from his lap. Her eyes jumped to his face and saw a slight nod and a tiny smile.

She knelt, her heart pumping volumes of blood to her head. She closed her eyes and waited. When Shep's hand touched her head, she thought she'd faint. A powerful wave, almost like electricity, swept through her body. His voice came echoing through a wind tunnel, blowing away all her doubts and fears.

"Deanna. One of the newest Lambs of the Flock. God has chosen you to be a missionary for Him. You will take your learning across the oceans to help those already there. This will not come to pass until you have received the crown of the True Lamb. And because of your advanced wisdom, you will begin training in six months rather than one year. You shall be great in the kingdom, Deanna. For God has spoken."

Deanna could not rise without help; her knees seemed glued to the ground with the power Shep had put through her.

Sharon helped her back to a spot on the grass. Her usual look of superiority had changed to a look of honor. Deanna grinned at her. Not in gratitude, as Sharon mistakenly believed, but in her own newly acquired superiority.

Jeff clutched the grass around him. Shep had his holy hands on Deanna. Jeff didn't think he could stand the joy that swept through him. Such a prophecy insured the chance of a future with Deanna. A close working relationship, if not more.

Jeff wished he could give Deanna a congratulatory hug right that instant. He felt his cheeks grow warm, when he realized he wanted to give her far more than a hug.

* * *

The bus ride home was too short for Deanna. The songs were not sung loud enough, and not enough joy could be squeezed out to adequately satisfy her. Never again would she be a nobody. Never again would she flounder in life, wondering what her purpose for living would be. She had been chosen for an eternal work. She lifted her chin and thanked God for choosing her.

$=10=$

Coming home from camp jarred Deanna into reality. The seediness of the boulevard glared against the perfect beauty of Green Pastures; smog choked the clean, deep breaths to which she had grown accustomed.

"Jeff, I want to go back to camp," Deanna complained. She sat on the green bench, and wiped her brow with an old raggy towel.

Jeff sat next to her, laying his tennis racquet on the bench. "Even though you'd be there without me?" he teased.

Deanna stuck her tongue out at him. "That was an awful shock you know. Why didn't you tell me they weren't going to let us even talk?"

Jeff leaned against the chain-link fence. "I didn't know what to do. I started to call you so many times. I wanted you there to learn about the Flock, to know how you'd respond. Then you looked so excited about going. . . . Then I thought it might not be that big of a thing." Jeff shook his head.

"No big thing? Thanks a lot. I thought I meant something to you."

Jeff bounced the tennis ball on the end of his racquet, trying to cover up his awkwardness. "I never had someone I cared about before. It never mattered that I couldn't talk with the girls." Jeff smiled at her. "Shep's talks made me feel like . . . well, like I had a direction to my life. That, I guess, is all I remembered. I wanted that for you, too."

Deanna touched his hand. "Thanks, Jeff. I *was* mad at first, but now I'm so glad we were separated."

Jeff frowned, Deanna laughed. "That's not as bad as it sounds. I know now, that the Flock has the answers for me, for the world. I will always be grateful to you for leading me into the truth." She leaned over and gave him a kiss on the cheek. Jeff closed his eyes, trying to ignore the sinful desires racing through his body.

He jumped up, flipping his racquet. "Come on, Deanna, we've got time for one more game."

* * *

For the rest of the summer, Deanna called Josie three times a day, and talked with Jeff once a day. She and Josie spent every other day together. They talked about camp, what Shep had taught them, and sang camp songs. She avoided Linda and Kathy, never returning their calls, even hanging up on them if she answered the phone.

Instead she went to the shopping mall with Josie, walking along with other kids their age, trying to get them to come to the next concert. They handed out hundreds of fliers, and even more smiles. They sold buttons for a dollar that read, I BELONG!

As the weeks passed, camp and the control it had over her life, started to drift to the back of Deanna's consciousness. Each Flock meeting roped her back with a jerk.

If she would have admitted it to anyone, she would

have said sometimes she thought she would go crazy with the conflicting thoughts that tortured her. She paced her room, she took long walks up and down the streets. She couldn't sit still for long. She tried to sort it out, but her mind seemed to be stuck.

The last week of summer she knew she would scream if she didn't talk to someone about it. Josie would have heart failure, Sharon or Carol or Reb would disown her from the Flock. Questions—the unforgivable sin. Jeff had been so busy lately, trying to study and prepare for his True Lamb ceremonies, that she only saw him at Flock meetings. His phone calls had dwindled. Besides, how could she talk about something so serious on the phone?

At Flock, she again felt like the lost Lamb. The one drifting without direction. She wandered through the mass of kids until she found Jeff. She touched his elbow. "Jeff, we've got to talk."

"About what?" he said cheerfully, waving at a friend across the room.

People closed in around them. Deanna shook her head. "Will you take me home tonight?"

"Sure. Isn't Josie supposed to?"

"Yes, but. . . ."

*   *   *

The waitress at Bob's seemed glad to see them. "I thought you two had split up or something. Two nice kids like you deserve each other."

"Thanks," Deanna said awkwardly. "I'll have a hot-fudge sundae."

"I'll have the same," Jeff said.

"Hmm, things *have* changed," the waitress remarked.

They poked around over weather and family news until the sundaes came. Then Deanna took one bite and unplugged the restrictions on her thoughts and fears.

"Something's weird, Jeff."

"Like what?"

"Like our Flock."

"What do you mean?"

"I can't put my finger on it. But ever since I came back from camp, my thoughts don't seem to be my own. Every time I try to think about something, Shep's words and image come to mind."

"That's terrific! I'm glad to hear that. That is the whole point of camp. To get you into a new method of thinking. Where your thoughts are no longer your own, but that of the Shepherd and of the Lord. I can't think of better things to think about than the Word of God, can you?"

"No, but there's something eerie about that." She suddenly lost all appetite for a sundae. She put the spoon on the dish and watched the ice cream melt with islands of fudge.

Jeff wiped the corners of his mouth. "You seem to be thinking okay right now."

"That's because I've been trying so hard to sort it all out. When I saw you tonight, I suddenly realized all you have meant to me, and how I've shoved it under a rug. It scared me to think that maybe we're drifting apart."

"I don't think we're drifting apart, Deanna. Our focus has just changed a little." Jeff gave her a big smile before shoveling in a spoonful of sundae.

Deanna couldn't look at Jeff. "Yeah. Now everything is focused on Shep and the Flock. I wonder if that's very healthy."

Jeff put his spoon down and leaned across the table. "What could be more healthy than to belong to a family that loves you? It's more than your own family has given to you. What could be more healthy than having a direction to your life? You didn't have that before you came to the Flock. Now your life also has eternal value."

Deanna bit her lip, then cocked her head. She considered carefully what he had said. She leaned back, the vinyl seat crunching. "So what about us?"

With not one moment of hesitation, Jeff answered her. "What about us? We are part of the same family, belonging to the same purpose. We'll be together always."

"Hmm." Deanna crossed her arms. "What kind of together?"

Jeff reached across the table and beckoned for her hand. He held it firmly in his own. "Deanna, I love you. I want to marry you. But first, we must give the Shepherd what he needs. We both must become True Lambs so that we can have the best possible union, if Shep agrees."

Deanna yanked her hand from him. "You sound like a squawking parrot . . . the best possible *union* . . . *if* Shep agrees?" Her voice began to stretch, cracking with the strain.

Jeff looked around to see if people were caught by Deanna's words. "Shep is the one who makes the matches. He knows us all better than we know ourselves, so he . . . uh . . . sort of decides who marries who."

"Well now, that just takes the cake. Don't I know who I love?"

"Shep listens to suggestions. He especially listens to the True Lambs," Jeff encouraged. "The more committed you are to God and to the work, the more Shep will listen to you."

"I think I've made a mistake, Jeff." Deanna gathered her purse and sweater. "I don't belong in this group. You're all little puppets being played by the master's hand."

Jeff put his arm out to stop her. "You made a promise, Deanna. Shep prophesied over you."

Deanna paused at the edge of the seat, then hung her head. "I know, Jeff. I'm just so confused right now."

Jeff smiled, concern pulling at the corners of his eyes and mouth. "That's a normal part of growing into the kingdom. Give it time. Listen to Shep with the ears of a child. For only a child will enter into the kingdom." Jeff hoped she believed him.

Deanna nodded. She swiped at her fluted glass and put her fudge-laden finger in her mouth. "All those camp experiences seem so far away."

"We must learn to live as Lambs in a world of wolves. We must stay together with other members of the Flock as much as we can. We will grow, and we will be used of the Lord."

Deanna cocked her head and looked intensely at Jeff. "Why do you sound a little different from the others? You always say Lord, and you pray in Jesus' name instead of in the name of the Shepherd."

Jeff's face turned the same shade of red as the cherry he had put in the ashtray. "Can you keep a secret? I'm only telling you because I assume you will be my wife one day and you will know anyway."

Deanna nodded.

"I read my Bible every day," he whispered.

"I thought you said Lambs don't need the Bible?" Deanna asked, leaning back into her seat.

"I can't get enough of it, Deanna. It's so addicting. The life of Jesus is so real, and His words to me so satisfying."

"More than Shep's?" she balanced purse and sweater on her lap.

Jeff sighed and put his head in his hands. "I don't know. But I do know that the more I read the Bible, the more I see Shep following the footsteps of Jesus."

Deanna leaned forward, putting her hand on Jeff's arm. "For you, Jeff—because of you—I will stay."

Jeff got up from the table and kissed her cheek. "You won't regret it, Deanna, I promise you. And I promise you, we'll convince Shep we're the couple of the century—when the time is right."

*   *   *

Deanna walked in confusion from the moment she woke in the morning until she went to bed at night. She didn't know what to do with her minutes, and felt lost in space—flailing about, reaching for support that wasn't there.

When Josie came over, or when she went to Flock, the feeling of falling stopped, as her new family surrounded her with a big quilt of love and acceptance.

Jeff came over three times a week, and they took walks to the park, passed out fliers at the mall, or played tennis.

One day, after a rough tennis match, Jeff wiped the sweat from his face with a stained towel. "Shep's watching me now, Deanna," he said in a soft voice.

"Why?"

"It's only six weeks until the True Lamb ceremony. My every move is monitored to be certain I am True Lamb material. They want no phonies, only the best."

"So no more tennis?"

"No, that's okay. The walks to the park will have to stop. I've also got some intense three-day workshops coming up. I may not get to see you much until school starts."

Deanna pushed her tongue in her cheek and tried not to cry. "I need your stability, Jeff."

"Keep praying, Deanna. Jesus will show you the stability you need."

Deanna longed to put her head on Jeff's chest, just for a moment, but she knew the serious consequences that would fall on Jeff if she did.

*   *   *

Stepping off a shuttle to Saturn could not have been as much shock to Deanna as going back to school in September. The kids were so . . . so, evil. Their language so sharp it stung her ears. She closed her eyes and chanted little verses she had learned at camp, to block out the scenes played around her.

Jeff had a spacey look in his eyes from the hours of studying for his True Lamb ceremony. Without Kathy and Linda, Deanna was a stranger in her own territory.

She tried to mimic Jeff's attitude of the previous year— smiling at everyone, being friendly, and inviting them to concerts. Her heart wasn't in it. Her heart was in her throat.

=11=

=Jeff sat nervously in the car, catching himself each time the car went around a corner. He wanted to lift his blindfold to scratch his eye, but knew it would be interpreted as trying to see where they took him. Twenty minutes passed before the car stopped. Once inside the building, his blindfold was removed.

He blinked his eyes several times, and rubbed the itch from them. He had never been to this building before. Without being fully aware of his actions, he moved his head about, trying to identify the sweet smell. Flowers and musk, he decided, not so strong to make him sick, but strong enough to make him heady.

At the entry table, sat a person Jeff had never seen before. The solemn man, dressed in a red robe, asked his name, and looked into a large book, bound in red leather, clasped with a locked leather band. He opened it, running his finger down columns of handwritten names. "Your name is found in the Shepherd's book of life. Congratulations."

A contagious smile spread over the bookkeeper's face. In spite of the bewilderment Jeff felt, he could not help but be relieved and smile in return.

The bookkeeper handed Jeff a key with a number on it. He was then directed to a small room filled with lockers. The lockers were not made of metal, but of wood. A rich mahogany, polished to a shine. Jeff matched his key to a number scrolled on the door. Opening it, he found white cloth garments; a floor length pullover shirt, and a white robe made of satin. He tied a white satin strip of cloth around his waist, and wore no shoes. For this was holy ground.

In a small anteroom, three women anointed him with oil—his ears, his lips, his nose, his eyes, his head, his hands, his feet. Jeff felt awkward and wanted to say something to them. He wanted to scream at them to stop, and run from the room. His inner conscience screamed that something was wrong. But he stood still and listened as the women spoke, their voices soothing and musical.

"This is to open the ears, to hear the Word of the Lord," said the beautiful one.

"This," said the blonde, her soft hair brushing his shoulders, "is so you will speak only the truth of the Shepherd, to all who will listen."

"This is to smell out the devil and flee his presence, or fight him, as is necessary."

"This is to open your eyes to all truth, and to perceive the place you are in."

Jeff wondered where these women came from, why their bodies smelled so clean, why they spoke so musically, yet so mechanically. It was as if he wasn't even there.

"This is to clear your brain of all that has come before, so that only that which the Shepherd says will be true."

"This is to anoint your hands in servanthood for the Savior."

"This is to anoint your feet, to travel and walk in the path of the Savior, the Shepherd."

When the anointing had been completed, they directed him to enter a room filled with Oriental rugs in tones of blue. The colors and designs brightened the room, making it comfortable, not frightening. Other True Lamb candidates were seated about the floor, heads bowed. Without being told to do so, Jeff sat and bowed his head.

Without looking up, he heard several more people come in. He wondered if their hearts beat as fast as his, gritting their teeth to keep their stomachs in place. Even with his eyes closed, he was aware of the lights dimming. A strange music wafted in the air. It could not be associated with any certain source, or any certain type. Jeff was sure it must be music of another country, another place, maybe even another world. Then voices started to speak, one after another, one overlapping another. Jeff tried to adjust his mind to take it all in, but it seemed impossible to concentrate on one thing.

"The Lord, He is good, His mercy endureth forever."

"Worthy is the Lamb that is slain."

"The Shepherd knows His sheep."

The words and the voices and some that sang comforted Jeff in his fear. Then one, repeated over and over, and starting small, then gaining volume and speed returned his fear in double measure. "They are His, and no one can snatch them from His hand." He wanted to figure out why this phrase, which used to be a comfort, now made him want to bolt from this place.

A voice, booming above the others said, "This is my beloved one in whom I am well pleased." As the voice faded, a light went on in the corner, to reveal Shep, kneeling by a rock. A light from above, slanted down, illuminating his face. On his face was a tear and beads of sweat.

His lips were moving, and suddenly, as if a microphone had been turned on, his voice could be heard.

"Oh, God, these are my sheep, my Lambs, who have come to give their all to You. Help me to lead them, even though I am so inadequate. Help them to become leaders of baby lambs and to know they are special, as no one else."

The lights dimmed again, making the room very dark. A door opened in one side of the room, and everyone got up and filed through.

In the next room, everyone was given lists of rules and behavior necessities for True Lambs. They were told verbally each one five times, in five different ways.

> A True Lamb does not question the Holy Word of God.
>
> A True Lamb does not question the words of our Shepherd.
>
> A True Lamb does not reveal the inner truths of this ceremony.
>
> A True Lamb does not reveal his new name, or his new date of birth to anyone but another True Lamb.
>
> A True Lamb keeps his body pure, abstaining from all physical contact with females.
>
> A True Lamb will obey with great joy.

A door opened to another room. As the True Lamb candidates stood to walk through it, they were separated. Reb appeared from a blackened door without a handle. He stood between two blue candles, the flickering lights bouncing shadows on his face. One at a time, each candidate knelt between the two candles, his head bowed before Reb. Reb spoke in a quiet voice, that no one could hear except the candidate. "Do you believe the Shepherd is God's one true leader, chosen of the Messiah to take His place and feed His sheep?"

Jeff swallowed, the words sticking somewhere deep inside. A verse from his Bible reading tried to break through, to make him defy the order and not say the words. If he had to say them, he would have choked. He cast out the negative thoughts as though they were Satan himself. He looked up into Reb's questioning eyes and said, "I do."

Reb smiled and put his hand on Jeff's head. "Now, my little Lamb. Receive the total freedom given only to those who know and follow the truth. You are now pure as He Himself is pure."

Jeff stood and walked through the next door, to face a panel of men he had never seen before. The door closed behind him and the men began to fire questions at him in rapid succession.

"To whom is the True Lamb's first devotion?"
"Does God allow evil to exist in the Flock?"
"Explain the Flock's doctrine in three sentences."

Five minutes melted into two hours. Jeff hated looking at the seven stern faces. Faces that looked determined to destroy him. No sooner had he begun to answer one question, than another was being stated. He had to avoid confusion. As abruptly as it began, the questioning stopped, and a helper led him from the room.

In the next room, he sat in a soft, blue chair. Every five minutes, another candidate came into the room and sat in one of the randomly placed chairs, until all ten were seated.

The moment the tenth arrived, they were plunged into darkness for three seconds before a screen lit up with the face of the Shepherd. He played a lute, his face serene and full of joy. As the camera panned back, sheep grazed around him. When his song ended, he stood from the rock and walked among the sheep. His hand, firm and gentle, touched each one. He said the name of each, and lifted their little faces to look at him. As the Shepherd moved, tears came to Jeff's eyes. He felt foolish, crying over such a thing, but the love of the Shepherd had finally reached his heart—that this Shepherd loved him in the same way he loved the sheep. He knew the hurting ones, and comforted them even more. He knew the strong, and was playful with them.

Jeff closed his eyes, and put his hand to his face. He thought of his unworthiness to know and be loved by a person such as this. When he opened his eyes, he saw something moving, creeping in one corner of the picture. The Shepherd sensed it too, standing and turning just as he saw the lion. Jeff watched in horror as the Shepherd ran toward the lion, shouting so the sheep would run in the opposite direction. The lion pounced. In a scene too vivid to describe, Jeff watched his Shepherd literally give up his life for the sheep. As the lion carted the torn carcass away, Jeff felt sobs bubbling from his throat.

The sound of sobbing took over the room as well as darkness. Someone lit a small candle in the corner of the room near the screen. Reb spoke softly, "The Shepherd gives his life for the sheep," and the candle went out.

A candle on the other side of the room flickered to life, and there stood the Shepherd. After so vivid a movie, the group gasped as one person. The Shepherd spoke: "My True Lambs. I have given my life for you, but I have come again so that you would not remain sheep without a Shepherd. Go now, into the world, and preach my words. Remember who you are and what you are."

The candle went out, and attention turned to Reb's candle, which had been lit again. "As you leave, you will state your new name and your new birth date to the keeper of the books. You will learn the secret handshake and be given your work assignment. All but the two still in school will report to work Monday morning. The remaining two may report to work Monday afternoon, one half-hour after school has let out. God bless you and keep you."

Jeff sat in silence, too stunned to move. The room emptied, and still he sat. His mind was certain he had left the world to enter into the kingdom itself. His heartbeat had slowed and his breaths came in long, deep, draws. His hands clasped, resting against his mouth, he stared into the darkness, still seeing the look of strength and peace on Shep's face as the lion devoured him. It made him sick. It made him weary. He forced himself off the chair and went to receive his work assignment and the secret handshake.

No one spoke or laughed, or even smiled in the locker-room. It was a moment of celebration, but the celebration was somber, and celebrated alone inside the individual mind.

At the front door, each was blindfolded again, and led to a car for the journey back to the basement where the Flock meetings were held.

*　　*　　*

The October heat mellowed into a cool autumn evening. Deanna strolled through the park. She had begged Jeff to meet her there following the five-hour True Lamb ceremony.

The shadows of the trees grew across the spiny grass. She stepped into the warm sand and trudged to the swings. She leaned the wrapped package against the pole, and sat in the warm swing.

Glad for the deserted park, she swung gently, her toes furrowing the sand.

A tall shadow crossed hers, and she twisted in the swing.

*　　*　　*

When the driver removed Jeff's blindfold, he blinked in the light of the setting sun. The car sped off before he could see who drove. He staggered to his mom's car, let himself in, and stared out the window. He laid his head back on the headrest, and it felt as though the whole car did a backward somersault. He opened his eyes quickly, but, no, it stayed on the ground.

He stared at the dash, trying to shift his mind into a mode where he could drive.

The next thing he knew, he was getting out of the car at the park, wandering to a form that swayed gently in a swing. Just before he reached her, she spun around. "Jeff!"

Jeff sagged in the swing next to Deanna's and clung to the chains. "Hi," he said feebly.

"What's wrong, Jeff?"

Jeff shook his head. "It's long, and hard, Deanna."

"What's it like?"

"I can't tell you. My head is buzzing with voices and promises and questions and answers. I want to go home and sleep. I think."

"I brought you a gift."

He raised his head with great effort. His eyes dull. "How nice."

Deanna hopped over to the package and put it in his hands. "It's for your birthday as well as a congratulations for such an achievement."

His hands moved heavily over the paper, pulling it off in shreds. She could see his eyes filling with tears when he saw the Bible commentary. "Now you can understand what each verse means," Deanna said.

"I'll like that, Deanna."

"I asked the lady what to get someone who was graduating into deeper commitment to God. She recommended it."

"I'm glad."

"You don't sound like it," she said gently.

"I know. I'm sorry. I'm a little confused. I think I should go get something to eat and go to sleep."

"Do you want me to go with you?"

Jeff managed a small, apologetic smile. "Thanks. But I

think I should be alone. I don't think I can manage one more minute of life. I need to hibernate."

"Will you be in school on Monday?"

Jeff shrugged his shoulders. "I don't really know, Deanna."

December 1

Red and black velveteen wallpaper ran down the walls into the carpet clumsily made to look like red and black tiles. Wrought-iron torches burned with flickering red light bulbs. A black-velvet painting of a toreador, his red cape lined with gold, flying in the air, hung above the long table. Nervous couples, all hovering around the age of forty-five, jiggled icy drinks and looked at the door of the restaurant in anticipation.

Twenty minutes later, the door opened. Shep walked in, his dark curls closely trimmed, his eyes that defied color definition, taking command of the room. He had purchased a brown tweed three-piece suit for the occasion. He approached each couple with a broad smile and an outstretched hand, surprising them by knowing their names.

He had a warm hug for both Jeff's parents. "Hey, it's been a long time since I've seen you two," Shep said warmly. "You're like family."

Jeff's dad slapped him on the back. "And you are most certainly a part of ours."

Shep turned away and stood at the head of the table. "Good evening, folks. I appreciate your asking me to meet you. I've missed seeing you at our monthly meetings for parents. Before we start, let's have a word of prayer."

All heads bowed, but not all eyes closed. Shep raised his hands in the air. "Oh, God, our Father," he thundered.

"Be with us now, in this room. Show us the truth, so the truth will set these worried folks free. In the name and power and glory of Your chosen One, *amen.*"

One of the women pulled a handkerchief from her purse and dabbed at the corners of her eyes. Most of the men, convinced their wives were overreacting, fidgeted with straws, or cleaned their fingernails.

Shep leaned forward on his hands, which rested on the table. "Who wants to start?" he questioned.

Mrs. Ranhill stood. "Sir, our daughter has been in Japan for seven months. We have not yet heard from her."

Shep's face looked concerned. "You have not heard from Sarah?"

"No, sir."

"I have had many letters from her. Have you had a good relationship with her?"

Mrs. Ranhill bristled. "Until you came along and planted lofty ideas in her head, yes."

"Perhaps this attitude is why you have not heard from your daughter. Next?"

"Sir," Mrs. Ranhill demanded. "I have received letters from Japan, but they are not from my daughter."

"How were they addressed?"

"Mom and Dad."

"Then I think, Mrs. Ranhill, that they must be from your daughter."

Mrs. Kling stood next to her. "I have received the same letter from my daughter."

Shep pushed his chin forward, perhaps trying to remember something about her. "Perhaps the work is so involved, the girls decided to write one letter."

"My daughter is in Argentina."

Unruffled, Shep raised his eyebrows. "My, what a coincidence."

Shep looked around the table, his eyes and words full of convincing power. "My friends. The work of God is time-consuming. I am sorry your children have chosen not to write. As for the coincidence of the similar letters, I must remind you that all our teaching is the same, whether it is taught in Japan, or in Argentina, or even in France or Germany. The words of God do not change for culture or language. It would not be surprising then that the letters are similar."

"Identical," Mrs. Kling corrected.

"Identical," Shep said with a smile and a nod. He continued. "I invite you to come see our offices. Come see the files we have on all our missionary posts throughout the world. You will see reports on the progress being made in each country. I have taken the liberty of bringing two reports with me." Shep nodded at a suited man standing in the back of the room. The man set a briefcase upon a chair, then removed two folders. He put one into the hands of the man at the head of each side of the table.

The anxious parents stood around the keeper of the folder, reading as best they could over the man's shoulder. Photos of happy, clean, young adults filled the folders. Photos of one or another teaching, or helping small children, or laughing in a group.

"How come," the mothers asked, "all this information is on countries where our children have not been sent?"

"I did not know who would be here tonight," the Shepherd said with calm assurance.

Jeff's mother spoke up. "I don't know most of you, but my son is a part of the Flock. My husband and I have been most grateful to Shep for the direction he has given our son." She looked at Shep who lowered his gaze in humility.

"Our son has never gotten into drugs, or any of the other evils his peers have. We have never had even one lick of trouble from him." She straightened her back and lifted her chin, looking haughtily around the room. "I can brag about him and his behavior every time my friends come over. None of *them* have problem-free children. *I* have no doubts about Jeff's involvement in the Flock. It has given me the freedom to go and be myself."

"Thank you, Mrs. Bradley," Shep said quietly.

The meeting continued for more than an hour. At the conclusion, there seemed to exist more confusion than before. Some of the people were convinced of the Shepherd's integrity, others, convinced of his deceit.

Nothing the doubters could say tripped Shep into an outright falsehood. The believers left the restaurant in small groups, marveling that this *might* be a man of God. His words, they agreed, as well as his conviction, and his power were all they admired in another human being. They agreed to end any investigation.

Only a few were left unconvinced by Shep's dramatics; yet without the support of their spouses, they did not know how they could fight Shep.

= 12 =

Jeff opened the commentary with reverence and caution. He knew such a book was forbidden by Shep, but it had a magnetism that he couldn't fight. Something about being able to read the verses and about how the Bible was written, anytime he wished, gave him the courage to disobey Shep.

He glanced around the room, as if Shep had eyes that could see him even then. He turned to John 10, Shep's favorite passage, because, he said, it spoke so clearly of himself, and the Flock.

Jeff read. He rubbed his eyes, and read again. He felt his chest rise and fall more rapidly. He read some more, then slammed the book shut. He squeezed his eyes closed, as if that would shut out what he saw.

In a moment, he became aware of a tremendous peace. He opened the book again, but this time, he stayed clear away from John. He opened to Genesis, to begin at the beginning.

Days and weeks melted into each other. School became a foolish necessity for both Deanna and Jeff. Deanna studied hard in math, and tried to involve herself in French. Shep had requested she learn it the best she could. The rest of the subjects she studied only enough to pass.

Her parents marveled at the change in their daughter. Once giving to everyone, she now focused all her energy on the Flock. It seemed all her generosity had evaporated. They might have been upset, except her rebellious behavior had disappeared. She did whatever they asked without comment. She didn't bug them with the silly talk that used to annoy them. The change was obviously for the better, they reasoned, so they kept quiet.

At Christmas, they had their first doubts.

"Mom, I can't take all the phony commercialism garbage. Can we do without a tree and lights, and just focus on the real meaning of Christmas?"

Mrs. Clark tossed a worried glance at her husband. "I don't know, Dee. I think your sisters want the traditional Christmas when they come home."

"I don't think it will hurt them," Deanna said with words so sugar-coated, it was amazing she didn't gag on them. "We dishonor Christ with all the sickening things we do at Christmas."

Mr. Clark cleared his throat, his temples throbbing in rhythm with his clenching teeth. Deanna knew he was ready to explode, and she didn't care. "We have never dishonored Christ at Christmas," he said, forcing control.

She looked him straight in the eyes and smiled real big. "Well, we never do much to specifically honor Him do we? And the only time I hear His name is in the songs you play on the records. I think we should have a real family Christmas. No gifts, just dwelling on the one, true gift."

"If this is the work of that group you're going to," Mr.

Clark roared, his fist landing on the table, making the silverware jump, "then you can just forget about ever going back."

"Dad," she said softly, piling on the sweetness. "I can't believe you would prefer a tree over the manger. Where do your priorities lie?"

"Priorities? Where'd you pick up a word like that?" Mr. Clark tossed his hands in the air. "The Shepherd, no doubt. That idiot!"

Deanna forced herself to keep smiling. Shep had warned them Satan would attack, and would use their parents to try to make them weak. She couldn't wait to move out. Away from satanic influence, and into the safety of the Flock apartments. She formed her words carefully, trying to remember as she memorized them in Flock the night before. "I have a program we can follow, Dad. It has all your favorite songs. We read lots of Scripture, and a real neat story written by Shep. There's programs for three days. Instead of celebrating Christmas on just one day, we can celebrate for three."

Mr. Clark stood and stomped out of the room.

Deanna closed her eyes and chanted soundlessly, "Out Satan, out Satan, out Satan, Shepherd's strength, Shepherd's strength."

Mrs. Clark, held out her hands and took Deanna by the shoulders. "What's the harm in what we've done all these years, Deanna?"

Deanna lifted her chin. "Plenty, Mom. We've got to change our ways if we are going to be honoring to God."

Mrs. Clark sighed. "Oh, all right. I'll talk to your father."

Deanna smiled the smug smile of one victorious.

*   *   *

Jeff stared at the "Recommendations for Flock Apartment Living" and swallowed hard. He wanted more than anything to slam his fist into the wall. But as a True

118

Lamb, he must swallow his questions and obey. How could he get frustrated with the plan and goodness of God Himself?

He unpacked his clothes, stuffing them into the rickety, unpainted dresser. He shivered, and turned up the heat on the old wall heater. It clicked and moaned protest, then sighed a gush of heat.

He put his pictures back into the boxes, following the guidelines posted on the wall. "Nothing is to be put on the walls except one mirror and one clock per room."

Glad his mother had taught him how, he awkwardly put sheets and blankets on the bed. He lifted the rotting curtain to look out into the January evening. It had been a small battle to get his parents to agree to the move. If his mom hadn't been so trusting of Shep, he didn't think he would have been able to pull it off with their blessing. He didn't really need their blessing; after all, he was eighteen.

Jeff leaped to open the door at the sound of the first heavy knock. "Hi, I'm Peter," said a tall Hispanic about twenty. "I thought I'd welcome you to our building."

"Thanks," Jeff said eagerly. "Come on in."

Peter's long steps took him to the couch, and he sat in a cloud of dust. He patted the cushion. "We are so lucky, aren't we?" he said in a thick accent. "The Shepherd takes such good care of us."

Jeff wanted to protest, but smiled. "Yes, he does."

Peter looked around the room. "Only a man of God would see the vision." He waved his arm in a great swirling gesture. "Apartments for his own, all over the world. So no matter where we are, we can be with those of our own kind. We do not need to live where others take the name of our holy God in vain, or watch the devil's television, or see the news of a perverted land. Here we can live in peace and true holiness."

Jeff felt he had entered a new country. The whole idea of living alone was odd enough. But he hadn't realized how much of the evil, sinful world he had accepted as okay. He mentally chastised himself.

"Peter, I wish I could offer you some lemonade, but I haven't had a chance to get to the store yet."

"Oh, don't worry, brother. There will be enough time for lemonade. Can I help you unpack?"

Jeff looked around hesitantly. "Well, there really isn't much to do. Shep provides everything except food and clothing." Jeff didn't want his new friend to leave; he sat on the edge of the overstuffed chair and looked into the friendly brown eyes. "I know how you can help me, Peter. I need to know where the grocery store is. You can help me shop—if you have the time."

"Of course I have the time!"

*   *   *

Deanna pushed herself into Saturday-morning meetings that taught precourses for those in training to become True Lambs. She and Josie giggled together all the way there, in every free moment, and all the way home again.

Deanna loved the meetings. They chased away all the doubt she had voiced in Bob's that night. Knowing the whole scope of the Flock, the holy purposes of which she would now be a part, erased any questions she ever had. She sat with her eager face always on the teacher. She filled notepad after notepad with scribblings of truth.

She appreciated their honesty. They even warned what others would say about the Flock. She was told that the jealous would call them a cult, to try to discourage others from believing. They would be told lies about Shep, claiming this humble man had hidden riches. They answered every question she ever had, without her even asking. Her mind seemed even to change its way of looking at the world. They bombarded her with love and words, and her mind joyfully molded itself to accept them.

She heard the talks repeated over and over until she

knew the shorter ones almost by heart. Her favorite talk though, focused on the man of her devotion—Shep.

The Shepherd, she learned, was a man with most of his past a secret. His father was a strict minister, his mother "the perfect example of submission."

As Reb spoke, Deanna fell into his words, and was carried by them. "The Shepherd's mother obeyed the words of the Lord, and her Lord, her husband. She never spoke a word against his work, or against his desires. She only adored him and followed him everywhere.

"As the Shepherd watched this marvelous expression of love and devotion, he thought of sheep and the adoring shepherd.

"Time and God led him to California, where he spent seven years studying God's Word in seminary. Yes, he spent more time in seminary than normal, because he had much more he wanted to learn. Then one day, on a trip to the mountains, God spoke to him in a small clearing in the midst of powerful redwood trees. There God told him that he had been chosen to lead His Flock out of the darkness and into the light."

Deanna shivered with delicious excitement. Josie reached for her hand and squeezed it. Tears filled both their eyes as Reb spoke more.

"But the Shepherd knew he was not worthy of such a high calling. He begged and begged God to find someone else. And the Lord said, 'There is none other on the earth, with a heart after Mine, into whose hands I can entrust My precious Lambs. It is you. You are the chosen. You must be the Shepherd.'

" 'But what will I say?' our Shepherd protested.

" 'You will say all that I tell you. I will teach you, and you will be My spokesman to all nations and to many generations.'

" 'What does that mean?' Shep had said, his face pressed against the grass. 'It means you are My prophet,' said the

Lord, His voice now quaking the earth. In tears, our Shepherd said in a tiny voice, 'Thy will, not mine be done, oh, Lord, my God.' "

The room was silent. Deanna felt her heart racing. *How special*, she thought, *to be in the presence every single week of the only living prophet of God. To have his words teach me. Oh God, please forgive me for ever questioning this man.*

The group broke for a small, quick lunch of cheese and crackers. Mounds of cookies dwarfed the offered cheese. Most of the kids ate handfuls of cookies and drank punch instead of eating the cheese and crackers. "I like to let others have my portion," Josie said to Deanna.

Within fifteen minutes, everyone was back in their places, munching quietly, and taking fervent notes again.

"I am sorry to have to take time on this next portion, little Lambs," Reb said with his face twisted in anger. "But the evil one is alive and strong, and we must be prepared to face him."

Deanna didn't look at Reb now. She wrote furiously in her book, trying to write down all the places Satan lived. Anyone not of the Flock taught Satan's ways. Her family, teachers at school, other kids. Everyone was an enemy that directed thoughts away from the Shepherd and the Flock.

"No one is safe from the evil one outside the Flock," Reb's voice boomed. "Only inside the Flock are you safe."

Deanna squirmed a little in her place, uncomfortable with the knowledge of being unsafe most of her days. No wonder she felt so much more comfortable with the Flock.

"For you who are still in school, you are there for a reason. God has put you there to bring others to the Flock. You are also there to learn as much as you can to bring skills into the Flock. For you, there is a special protection. But that protection isn't foolproof. You can still be led astray by your own foolish desires."

Deanna blushed, thinking how hard she had pushed Jeff to stray from the Flock. She made a note to ask God and Jeff for forgiveness.

*   *   *

"Deanna, Kathy has called three times this week. Why don't you call her back?" Mrs. Clark asked her.

Deanna slid the plates onto the table, added the glasses and silverware. "It's not important anymore, Mother."

"What do you mean it's not important anymore? The only friend you made at school is home for spring break, and it's not important to see her?"

"No, Mom, it's not." Deanna held her head up, standing straight and tall, smiling smugly at her. "There are more important things in life than silly games of tennis, chitchat about boys and school. I don't care to waste my precious time with people unconcerned about the condition of the world."

Mrs. Clark closed the oven and pulled the mitt off her hand. "Deanna! I'm getting tired of this self-righteous attitude of yours."

"I'm not self-righteous, Mother."

"Then why do you snub anyone not connected with the Flock?"

"They pull me down, Mom. I never knew what a joy it was to serve the Lord. My life is now His. I have important work to do, and I'm not going to waste any minutes of my time with idiots who refuse to see the truth and follow it. Time is running by fast, Mom, and one day people will wake up and see they were wrong, and it will be too late."

Mrs. Clark whirled around toward the stove, her frustration tightening every muscle in her body. She closed her eyes and shouted, "It's this Flock that's made you like this. If it was really a good thing, you wouldn't be so awful."

Deanna slammed the last fork onto the table. "Perhaps you are the awful one, Mother."

*   *   *

Deanna looked around the crowded basement, trying not to be too obvious. When she saw Jeff, her heart picked up its beating. She wiped her palms on her pink cotton pants, and wandered casually in that direction. She knew that missing him was improper behavior for a True Lamb. But she wasn't a True Lamb yet. That was only a couple of months away. Still . . . .

His curls, always wild, gave the impression he could not be tamed. She sometimes wondered if the Flock had really tamed him. When he saw her, he smiled. Her favorite smile. She'd never seen him smile that way for anyone else. With his braces gone now, he looked like a new person.

"Jeff, how are you?" she tried to ask as if she simply stumbled by.

He looked at her. Did she detect a loneliness? A longing for something? For her? "Hi, Deanna." Very aware of those listening, he said words he wouldn't have said if they had met on the street. "How is your True Lamb training?"

"Good, Jeff. How come I don't see you in school anymore?"

"Shep arranged for an early graduation. I took the equivalency test and passed. He needed me to start work right away."

The people around them drifted away. Deanna let something bubble up from some stuffed place inside. "I never see you anymore," she whispered. "How come you don't call? I miss you."

Jeff looked down. "It's the guidelines of the apartment, Deanna. And of. . . ." He looked up, startled at what he almost said. "You will know soon," he said.

Deanna nodded. "Can we sit together at Flock and to-night—and all the other concerts?"

Jeff leaned over to whisper in her ear. "Don't make it obvious, but yes,"

In honoring and respecting their common goal and commitment, they still found a way to see each other. During the concert, Deanna's hand again rested by her side. Jeff's rested by his side, and if anyone had looked closely enough, they could see fingers touching.

$=13=$

$=$**J**eff sat at his desk, flicking tiny pieces of paint from the wood with a pin. He hoped to refinish his desk. He tired of getting splinters in his hands when he wrote in longhand. He let his mind drift; as it did, it floated to where it always went: Deanna. He thought of the way she cocked her head when she listened intently to anyone. He thought of the way she smelled, the way she spoke and laughed.

The phone rang, and he had to shift his brain to Spanish.

* * *

Deanna thought less and less for herself. And more and more her thoughts were carved, molded, and suggested by the Shepherd. Her smile became a permanent fixture on her face.

Three hours a day, she spent listening to Shepherd tapes, memorizing Scripture and Lamb Guidance.

Deanna especially liked Lamb Guidance. From the booklets she learned how to talk to others—what to say, what not to say, what questions to ask, and when to ask them. She memorized the order, as encouraged by Shep, so when visitors came to concerts or Flock meetings, she could bounce up to them and make them feel welcome. They taught her when to hug someone, or give them a shoulder squeeze. They taught her how to tell small lies to encourage people to come back. "All methods are righteous when bringing people to the kingdom."

So Deanna told them she loved them, that they were *incredibly* special, or that the Flock owned and supported a children's home, or anything she felt would draw them back another time.

Deanna felt most comfortable with the other Lambs, the least comfortable at school or at home. At home, there was no one to help her chant verses, or pray when Satan prowled, ready to attack. She felt his presence when the television blared, when her parents were home, when she was alone in the bathroom. Satan knew her vulnerable moments, and she had to be ready at all times.

She referred to Lamb Guidance whenever she had a decision to make. She never wanted to make a wrong decision, for that could take you out of God's perfect will forever. She relied on Shep's wisdom for all things. She now bought most of her things at stores where Flock people worked. Shep owned many of them, therefore those things the stores carried were blessed, and no longer carried the threads of Satan in the clothing, or the beads of poison in the food.

*   *   *

Jeff stared at his Bible commentary. It was happening again. The commentary couldn't be right. He looked back at his Bible, and started rocking back and forth, praying frantically for God to tell him the truth. He wiped the sweat off his forehead, flipped through a stack of booklets, and took out Lamb Guidance booklet number five. He turned the pages slowly but impatiently. Page thirty-six. The last page. He checked it with the Bible and with the commentary.

He slammed the commentary closed, and heaved the heavy book across the room. A massive headache pressed on his forehead, and he pressed it back. He prayed and prayed for truth, rocking, rocking. He stood from his knees and left the apartment. Walking on the boulevard, the cars sped past, blowing dirt caught from the street. Jeff walked until he could push the words he had seen to the back of his throbbing head.

*　　*　　*

The Flock sagged under the absence of their leader. The Shepherd had so much work to do in his Flocks around the world. He left more of his work to Reb, trusting him to be the guard of the Flock while the Shepherd was away.

Deanna served punch to the Lambs and to the newcomers who wandered around looking confused and bewildered. She laughed, thinking of how she looked as lost as they, her first weeks at the concerts.

A hush spread across the room. The crowd hung together, then parted, in a rippling motion.

Deanna dropped the ladle in the punch as the smooth voice reached her. "Deanna, my little Lamb." She looked into the adoring face of the Shepherd. At first fear strangled her, then melted away as the power of love conquered her fear.

Shep touched her hand, and gently led her from behind the punch bowl. He looked her over, making her feel uncomfortable and very lovely all at once. He stroked her arm, then kissed her hand, his kiss lingering there. She felt heat race up her neck and into her face, pricking like needles under her arms.

"It will not be long before you are a True Lamb, and a worker for the Flock. You are a beautiful Lamb, Deanna."

Beyond Shep, Deanna saw on Jeff's face a mixture of
anger and confusion. She glared at him, then turned a
soft smile to Shep. "Thank you, Shepherd. It will be an
honor."

Shep stroked her face with the back of his hand. "We
must get a photograph of you soon, to send to the mission
fields. I think you will be in high demand."

Deanna grinned proudly at his words. "I will work hard
to win more Lambs to the Flock."

*   *   *

The office buzzed with activity. More missionaries would
leave by the end of the week. Passports had to be finalized
as well as visas and inoculations secured. The missionaries
came in flurries of excitement and questions.

Jeff loved his part in the machinery. He soothed fears,
answered questions, and made many phone calls. He
caught all the phone calls from the mission fields of France
and Spain, and any of the Latin countries. Someday he
hoped to go himself. The Shepherd promised he would.
To think he had a part in the salvation of those around the
world brought a smile to his face every time he thought
about it.

During a quick walk down the hall and back, he marveled that he, Jeff Bradley, could have such a vital place in
God's work. At home, he was the kid of his parents'
dreams, but there was no purpose in that. Here he had
more than purpose. He had a holy destiny.

As he sat in the chair, he caught sight of the yellow
Happy Face poster on the wall. WE SACRIFICE FOR JESUS, it
said. Jeff could think of nothing he wanted more, than to
have his life sold out for Jesus. And in this place blos-
somed the manifestation of it all.

After five months in the Flock apartment building, he
could imagine living nowhere else. His new roommate
kept him from getting lonely. They discussed Lamb
Guidance at all hours of the day or night. Daily, the

apartment occupants on each floor gathered to study Lamb Guidance, to listen to Shep's tapes, to discuss them, and encourage each other. Never had he felt such a sense of family.

The women's apartment building was on the opposite side of the street. They often had good-natured jokes and gags between them. At least once a week, a long sign on butcher paper hung out the window of each building as a message to the other.

WE ARE LAMBS, MUTTONCHOP!
GOD LOVES YOU
AND SHEP DOES TOO

As the heat built up inside, water balloons occasionally came sailing through an open window.

In the all-alone moments, in the middle of the night, Satan attacked Jeff with questions and thoughts of Deanna. He quoted his Scripture over and over, until at last, he fell into chaotic dream-filled sleep.

* * *

Samuel brought in a stack of photographs and dropped them in Jeff's IN box. "All these are marked with languages, Jeff. Your input should smooth things out. Let me know which ones you need extra copies of, and I'll make them up right away."

"Thanks, Samuel."

He picked up the stack of photographs, thumbing through the top five. Not one of the girls could be considered ugly. Each was cute, adorable, or downright gorgeous. "God chooses beautiful women to be his missionaries," Shep had said. He wasn't kidding.

Jeff knew most of the girls. Josie, he knew, would never be one of them. Carol had gone last month to France, with two others.

He placed the pictures upside down, to organize them

by the languages they knew, paying no attention to the names. Those with more than one language would be sent to a country whose language they did not yet know. They would pick up the language easily. Those with only one language must go to a country in which that language was spoken.

As Jeff scooped up the piles, he stopped. *Deanna Clark*. He flipped the picture over. Deanna's head was cocked to one side. Her hair blew behind her, her eyes wide with anticipation, as if she just stepped off the plane in her new country. Jeff dropped her picture in his drawer, between some files. He slammed the drawer shut, and got back to work.

*   *   *

Deanna lied to her mother about where she planned to go. Her mother would lock her in her room if she knew what Deanna was about to do. The lie didn't bother Deanna at all. She was about to become a True Lamb.

Having a tendency to become carsick did not help her already excited stomach during the blindfolded drive to the ceremony building.

During the anointing, her butterflies and nausea left her. She felt honored, a queen, a vital importance to someone. The ceremony did not bewilder and confuse her as it did Jeff. She sat in holy awe, knowing that for the first time in her life, she was doing something right. She was more than just an excess human on the earth. Her life had more value than her sisters'—more value than the kid's next door. She was valuable to God, and that made all the difference in the world.

When the rules and necessities for True Lambs were stated, her thoughts took her back to camp, where each one poked her and made her rebel. Now she smiled at them, thankful for the way they helped her remain in the truth.

A True lamb does not question the Holy Word of God.

I won't.

A True Lamb does not question the words of our Shepherd.

Never.

A True Lamb does not reveal the inner truths of this ceremony.

It is too precious to throw before swine.

A True Lamb does not reveal his new name, or his new date of birth to anyone but another True Lamb.

I won't.

A True Lamb keeps her body pure, never sharing it with anyone.

Deanna blushed, remembering how she had thrown herself at Jeff. *I will obey this rule,* she said to herself firmly, kicking away the thoughts Satan wanted to feed her. *How dare he attack me here, where all is holy and pure.*

A True Lamb will obey with great joy.

I will obey ALL commands, she stated to Satan firmly.

When Deanna stepped back into the car, her blindfold securely fastened, she thought she had never felt such joy. Ever. She never once got queasy on the way back.

*   *   *

Deanna's sisters stared at her. Her mother's eyes filled with tears, her father shook his head. "But *why,* Deanna?"

her mother pleaded. "I've waited all your life for this day, and you don't even want to acknowledge it."

"Mom, graduation doesn't mean anything anymore. Not graduation from high school. The only graduation I care about is my graduation to a higher plane of holiness."

"It sounds like a higher plane of stupidity," her father mumbled. Deanna shot him a dirty look.

Claire put her fork down on her plate. "Deanna, this means a lot to Mom and Dad. Can't you go through with it for them?"

Deanna sighed. "I have to do what's right for me, Claire. That's what I hear you tell Mom and Dad all the time. This is right for me. I would be a hypocrite if I pretended I was all sad and everything over leaving the school. I'm not sad. I hated every minute this past year. If it wasn't for Shep, I wouldn't have gone at all."

"I suppose Shep told you not to go through with this," Dawn accused.

"No one told me anything," Deanna said firmly. "It was my own decision."

Claire leaned forward in her seat and stared hard into Deanna's eyes. "Do it for Mom, please? Can't you see how much this means to her?"

Deanna mimicked her sister's position. "Can't you see how much this means to *me?* No one has ever respected *my* decisions. I've always had to listen to a crowd of lousy sisters who think they are my counselors. Well, this time I make *my* decision and no one's going to change that."

Deanna received her diploma in the mail two weeks later. She ripped it into tiny pieces and dropped them into the kitchen trash.

*   *   *

Jeff stared at the check. He had never seen one so large. One hundred twenty thousand dollars. The designation was in Spanish. "Six at twenty thousand American dollars." Six *what?* What had Shep sold? The word *drugs* popped in his mind. *Foolish. Why would Shep be selling drugs to Colombia? That would be the other way around.*

He shoved the check back into the envelope and put it at the bottom of his stack of mail. He would pretend he never saw it, channeling it, instead, back to the bookkeeping room where it belonged.

He also chided himself for thinking such horrible things of his Shepherd.

He finished opening the mail, pleased to have received three letters from missions in Japan, Colombia, and France. The new missionaries sent home words of progress.

He saved them all until last. He opened the one from France, their newest mission field. Jeff's old friend Chandra had been sent there, and the letter had been signed by her.

Dear Family,

Thank God for our Shepherd. He was so wise to send us here. We already have ten converts . . . new baby lambs, ready and eager to learn of Him who sent us. Few are called, few are chosen. We must reach out, for the time is short.

Many blessings,
CHANDRA

Jeff smiled, his joy boosted with the letter.

His joy crashed into the agony of one betrayed when he read the next two letters. For aside from the postmark and the signature, the letters were identical. The same typewriter had been used for each one, as the *h* was missing a piece of its hump, making it look like an *l* with an *i* set too close.

Jeff swallowed hard. Ugly, sick thoughts came to mind. Was the check for six *women*? Six of Shep's precious Lambs? He clenched his teeth, forcing the thoughts out of his mind.

Jeff folded the letters, and took them out to Shep's box. Shep would read them at the next Flock meetings, one every couple of weeks, so no one would notice the similarity.

Jeff looked up as if to plead with God, then looked away.

=14=

=Deanna felt a piece of paper being shoved underneath her fingertips. She tightened her fingers around it. When the singing and clapping started, she opened it in her lap, singing and swaying with the others until the paper lay flat. She glanced at it during the prayer.

Meet me at Bob's, in the back, after Flock. PLEASE.

Another song, this time, sung standing up. The Lambs stomped their feet and clapped their hands. Deanna looked up at Jeff and nodded slightly.

In the darkened corner of Bob's, Jeff hid behind a menu. Deanna slid next to him. "I almost didn't see you. I had to come all the way around the corner to see even that someone was back here. Why all the secrecy?"

"You know why, Deanna."

"Well, I still think it's silly. No other True Lambs would be caught dead in a public restaurant. You don't have anything to worry about." She tapped the table impatiently. Jeff looked at her once neatly groomed nails and swallowed his words. They were still very clean, but they were clipped short, instead of filed and painted. He closed his eyes, then opened them to Deanna's stare. "What's wrong, Jeff?" she asked unkindly.

"Something's wrong with the Flock, Deanna. Something I can't put my finger on." Jeff gulped, his eyes bulging with fear of Deanna's reaction.

Deanna squinted her eyes and leaned over the table. "Have you been talking with someone you shouldn't, Jeff? This isn't like you. Of course there's nothing wrong with the Flock. What's wrong is with the rest of the world, especially America. Too many people with too much money, and no concern for God's chosen people."

Jeff cleared his throat. "So you have no doubts that Shep is the chosen one of God?"

"Of course not, silly. And neither do you."

"But there's something about the missionaries that's fishy."

"Like what?"

"Like they're mostly all women."

"Shep has explained that. He trained his staff long ago, and sent them to make a place before he sent the women. He takes care of his women as weaker vessels. He would never have sent any woman without establishing the organization first with trained male staff."

Jeff shook his head. "It still seems strange that they rarely add to the male staff. In only three places in the world do the numbers of the Flock seem to be growing. In the ten other places we send the beautiful missionaries, the numbers don't grow. At least not by much. And then, the growth is in the numbers of adult men, not children, or kids like us."

Deanna shrugged her shoulders. "It doesn't bother me."

"And we never hear from the girls in those places again."

"Sure we do. We get letters every once in a while. Gosh, Jeff. They are so busy, how can you expect them to have time to write? God's work doesn't allow time for frivolous activities like writing letters."

Jeff felt a tearing inside. Wanting to believe, knowing she was right, and another part of him screaming, as a trapped man would scream for life. The whole conversation seemed to go nowhere and he couldn't express what he wanted to say.

Deanna reached across the table and put her hand on his. "Don't question," she implored him. "It will only let Satan have a chance to confuse you. You know what is right. Stick to it. Don't question. Go home and study your Lamb Guidance. You'll feel better."

"I've been reading my Bible, Deanna. And the commentary you gave me. I know I shouldn't, but I can't help it. It's fascinating." His voice dropped to a whisper. "But some of the things it says are so opposite the things Shep says."

Deanna shook her head. "I should never have bought you that commentary, but I did it before I knew better. The Bible and Shep's words are not opposite each other. They are one and the same. If anything is wrong, it's the commentary."

Jeff thought Deanna looked like all the other little "mothers" running around the Flock. Her finger scolded with her wagging tongue. All at once he realized how alone he had become. Alone in a big, happy family called the Flock.

*   *   *

He had never cried so hard for so long. The top of his head hurt, his tears stung his face. He confirmed his eyes were as red and swollen as they felt, when he looked into the mirror.

If ever a hurt went deeper than betrayal, he didn't know what that could be. To trust someone so deeply, so completely, and then to have that trust irrevocably broken. It was not a trust bent by misunderstanding. It was a trust shattered by the ugly truth.

His sluggish heart beat on in his chest, but he wished it wouldn't. He wished somehow that the heart would stop, and he would drift off into oblivion. He didn't care about forever anymore.

He put his head in his hands and rubbed the skin around his eyes.

He could go on. He could continue in his work. After all, wasn't the Shepherd God's chosen one? Then did God allow evil, even *use* evil to complete His work on earth?

Jeff had taken his questions to Reb. Reb had said that the methods didn't matter, the outcome did. And weren't many more people coming to the kingdom? Many more trusting in God? And then Reb had looked at him closely, demanding to know if Jeff really meant those questions, because if he did. . . .

A battle raged inside Jeff's soul. The one side insisting that if Jeff left the Flock, his soul would rot in hell. Satan would win the battle. He had no friends outside the Flock.

A quiet voice gently urged him to leave the evil behind. That it couldn't be God's way to ship women across the sea to fulfill the pleasures of foreign men. *Some people would call that white slavery.*

Jeff uncrumpled the wad of paper in his hand. He pulled another from the trash, flattened it and set the two next to each other. He tried to rationalize the figures as living expenses for each so-called missionary. But thirty-five thousand dollars a woman was more than enough for anyone living in a poor country. And the signatures were the agreements for *particular* women—women whose photos Jeff had sent to those countries.

Jeff shook his head, sobs coming from inside. How many "missionaries" had he approved? How many had he sent, unknowing, like lambs to the slaughter? He wanted to tear his hair at the absurdity of his acceptance of the explanations given him. The chair creaked as Jeff leaned back in it, and kicked his feet up on the desk. He crunched the pencil between his teeth, and spit the pieces in the trash. "You only need one set of clothes. There are plenty of clothes, fit for a bride, once you get there."

Jeff remembered two of the letters passed to him by mistake. Intended for Shep and Reb, the letters contained degrading remarks about the "brides" having arrived. Jeff had stared horrified, at the "Missionaries" dressed in exquisite gowns, their faces more fitting for a funeral than a wedding. Their bodies slumped, their hands limp at their sides. A farce.

But God's Word *was* being taught in other places. The transforming of minds as Romans 12:2 spoke of: *And do not be conformed to this world, but be transformed by the renewing of your mind. . . .*

Minds were being transformed. Transformed into the image of God through Shep. Jeff could stand back and see how the minds were changed from thinking ones to dependent ones. He watched Deanna's and Debbie's, and Paul's and Steve's—and so many others.

Jeff broke another pencil in two, and sat up straight again. He crumpled the papers, and tossed them in the trash with the pencil.

"Hi, Mom," Jeff said hesitantly into the phone. "How're you and Dad doing?"

"Oh, Jeff! It's been so long since we've heard from you. Oh, wait. It's my turn to bid."

Jeff heard her hand slide over the receiver, and her muffled voice. Then, "When are you going to come by and see us?"

"I don't know, Mom. I'm a little upset about things here."

"What? Upset? How could you be? With a wonderful

leader like Shep, how could anything be wrong?" Jeff thought he heard her voice begin to tremble. The next sentence sounded almost like a plea. "Just talk to him about it, dear. I know he'll help."

"I don't think I can. I think he's doing something illegal, Mom."

"Jeff! How dare you say that! We've known Shep ever since he came to Parkside. He's never done anything except show the most exemplary behavior. Don't you dare say anything wrong about him. Now you just trot off to that apartment of yours, or to your office, and forget all this nonsense. I've got to pay attention to this game, or Lois and I are sure to lose."

Click!

Jeff stared at the wall, not believing his mother's attitude. "Dear God, what am I going to do?"

A thought popped into his head. He reached for the phone again and stopped. He dropped the receiver back into the cradle. He dug around in his desk drawer and found a rubber band. He popped it into his mouth and chewed. He swiveled a moment in the chair, and reached for the phone again.

"Good afternoon, Parkside Presbyterian Church."

"Ahem, um, could I please speak with Pastor Jim please?"

"May I tell him who's calling?"

"Jeff Bradley."

"Just one minute please."

Jeff started being aware of his breathing and his heart stepping up the beats.

"Yes, Jeff!" Pastor Jim's voice boomed happily across the line. At that moment, Pastor Jim sounded far away.

"Uh, Pastor Jim, I'm with the Flock, you know, with Shep—I mean Mitch Campbell. . . ."

Pastor Jim's voice became very solemn. "I know. I was sorry to hear that."

"You were?" Jeff heard a tiny click, and Pastor Jim's voice came in loud and clear. Jeff felt a throbbing in his ears.

"Yes, Jeff. I've heard of some problems . . . well, we shouldn't talk about it on the phone. Perhaps we can meet somewhere?"

The door to Jeff's office opened and Reb came in and sat down in the wooden chair across from Jeff. All the doubts fled Jeff, while a firm resolve and new knowledge took over. "I think I've changed my mind. That won't be necessary." Without waiting for a response from Pastor Jim, he hung up the phone.

Reb's stern face moved into a smile. "You are doing the right thing, Jeff. 'All things work together for good to them that love God and are called according to his purpose.' You are called to work in this area of His plan. 'For He who created you for this purpose is God.' Anyone as committed to the Flock as you will be blessed with greater responsibility in the kingdom."

Jeff felt the warm glow of appreciation spread through him.

Then an ugly look passed over Reb's face. "And if you ever turn from the Flock, if you ever talk to anyone about our inner workings. . . ." Reb's face turned a bright red. He stood, tapping the desk lightly with his knuckles. "Just remain loyal, Jeff."

*　　*　　*

For the first time, Deanna didn't hear the Lamb Guidance lesson. She couldn't forget the weird things Jeff had said three nights before. The dark circles under his eyes had grown deeper, his shirt seemed to hang on him instead of fit. She absentmindedly doodled on her notebook. Should she report him? It was required of all True Lambs to report those who seemed to be straying into Satan's domain. Those reported were taken to an unspecified place where they stayed for four months. No one knew what went on there, but when they came back, they never questioned again. They also could be compared to a cabbage.

Deanna couldn't do that to Jeff. She knew he'd come around in time. But she was afraid he'd sink his own ship if he wasn't careful.

After the meeting, True Lamb Gina approached her. Her right eye twitched. Deanna had gotten used to it, and was no longer distracted by it. "Why haven't you gone to the mission field yet?" Gina asked her.

"I'm not sure," Deanna replied. "Jeff said it has nothing to do with my lessons, or me, it's just hard to find a match."

"Oh. I sure wish I was called to the mission field. But I'm going to be a secretary for Reb, instead." Gina sighed, and pushed her stringy hair behind her ears. "I don't suppose you could get Jeff to change things for me?"

Deanna shook her head. "He doesn't decide who goes. God does. Jeff just matches missionaries with outposts." Deanna laughed. "If I can't even get him to work faster to get me going, then how do you think I can get you a missionary status?"

Gina nodded, not comprehending well. "Oh. Well, could you ask him anyway?"

"Okay, Gina."

*   *   *

Deanna watched Jeff's face as he played with a rubber band. "Can you do it?"

"No, I can't. That's up to God and Shep," Jeff said, his voice flat.

"And what about me? Why haven't I been assigned?"

"It takes time."

Deanna cocked her head and looked at him. He refused to meet her gaze. "Then why has the second group already gone, and I'm the only one remaining from the first group?"

Jeff shrugged his shoulders.

"Jeff, you don't understand how much this means to

me. All my life I've been a nobody in a world full of some-bodies. Now I have the chance to be someone important. A chosen woman in the chosen line of the Flock. Chosen by the Shepherd of God. Righteous, with holy and impor-tant eternal works. Don't deny me this chance, Jeff. Please."

Jeff opened his mouth, a mute plea. Reb came in the office. "Is there something wrong?"

Jeff looked at his desk, Deanna turned to him. "It's just a delay in my assignment, Reb. I've come to see if Jeff can hurry it up."

Reb looked at Jeff. "What kind of delay, Jeff?"

Jeff sighed. "There is simply no assignment yet."

"I can hardly believe that. Let's be certain no personal feelings are standing in the way of the Shepherd's Work. I expect her to be assigned within two weeks."

"Yes, sir."

Deanna was elated. She couldn't understand why it seemed Jeff had tears in his eyes.

*　　*　　*

Jeff felt creepy, as if the tiny hairs on his back were stand-ing on end. He turned around, but there was nothing behind him. He continued on his walk home. He held his heavy bag of groceries to his chest. In the store he kept running into a heavy-set man who looked at him care-fully—as if trying to see inside his brain. The whole inci-dent made him feel uncomfortable.

Jeff turned again. He thought he saw the edge of a coat sleeve, as someone darted into a doorway. He felt relieved to arrive at his apartment.

= 15 =

houghts smacked against brick walls, reeled, and tried another direction. Jeff wanted to shake his head, and somehow rattle them into place, into orderly control. Even though the thermometer pushed ninety outside, he sipped the hot coffee, the ceramic mug shaking in his nervous hand.

Pastor Jim clasped his hands, and leaned forward on the desk. "It's not just Christians who categorize the difference between a cult and an honest religion, Jeff."

Jeff bolted upright. "The Flock is not a cult. It is the chosen group of God. We must follow Him alone, to rectify the faults of society. The Flock will grow until we replace society as you know it today."

Jim nodded understanding, not agreement.

"We are the one true Church. You should come to a meeting sometime, Pastor Jim. We sing a lot of the same songs as you do. We memorize verses. Each True Lamb knows four hundred verses by heart, and learns more each month. Do any of your people know that many?"

Jim ignored the last question. "Mitch, I mean, your Shepherd, would not allow me to attend any of your meetings. I would be kicked out."

"That's not true," Jeff pleaded.

"Your Shepherd will not allow anyone in leadership from another church to attend your meetings," Jim said sadly.

"It must be because you are so steeped in the ways of Satan that he does not feel there is any hope of your turning back," Jeff defended.

Jim failed to stop the chuckle that bubbled up from inside. Jeff turned his body away, and looked toward the tall window. "Jeff," Jim said gently. "You know me. You know me very well. Has my life been one that exudes the evil you talk about?"

Jeff didn't answer, or turn back to look at Jim.

"A person's faith is made visible by their works. What have mine been?"

Jeff stood and walked to the window. He lifted the sheer curtains and looked down at the parking lot. A man stood under a tree, standing on one foot, and then another. He turned his left arm to look at his watch. He crushed his cigarette under his foot, and walked away.

"The Shepherd's works have been many and marvelous. His people have zeal and confidence. We have something more than you do. Something more than the socialites who march in and out of your church every Sunday. If we are to compare works, yours are like that of a five-year-old child in comparison to a master."

"I'll agree with that," Jim said, taking Jeff by surprise. Jeff stared at him as Jim continued. "Mitch is certainly a master. A master at what he does."

"Then you agree with me?"

"I didn't say that. I said he is a master at what he does."

Jeff wandered back and sat on the edge of the chair. "Then what do you mean?"

"I don't want to say right now. I want you to leave here, and I want you to open your eyes and be aware. I want you to notice some things about the Lambs. How often is there humor, teasing, or silliness among them?"

"I can tell you right now, there is none. That kind of behavior is of the devil. We smile and laugh during the songs which require it as worship to the Lord. But we do not engage in such things alone. That would be wrong."

Jim raised one eyebrow and continued. "I also want you to be aware of how many are sleepy and hungry. How many use their own intelligence to make a decision."

"I can already answer those. Satan attacks with sleep and hunger to get our minds off the Shepherd. We must deny those things because that would be giving in to Satan's lure. Those things take away our time to serve.

"We make decisions based on what Shep would have us do. We do things at the same time, for there is strength in unity. There is nothing wrong with being of one mind. The Bible even encourages it."

Jim smiled. "Will you think about those things, and be aware of them? And will you come back to see me next Saturday at the same time?"

Jeff tapped his empty mug, silent for a moment. He was about to say no when he looked up at Jim, and saw something in his eyes that drew him. "Okay. Three o'clock."

"Right."

*   *   *

Deanna stuffed a shoe into the last box, and tucked in the flaps. She smiled, then kicked the canopy bed. "I hope this is the last I see of you," she told it. Josie ran in and smacked her hands together. "Okay, the car's full. I don't know how in the world we'll get that last box and us jammed in there. Let's go!"

Deanna couldn't talk the whole way to the apartment

building. It wouldn't have mattered anyway since Josie's mouth never seemed to stop. Deanna could only think about finally escaping the clutches of Satan, and huddling into the protection of the fold. As expected, her mom had pleaded, her dad yelled. It didn't make one drop of difference to Deanna. She simply closed her ears to the protests by chanting a verse over and over, smiling the whole time.

Her parents weren't home to say good-bye. She purposely hadn't told them exactly when she'd be leaving. She didn't even tell them where she planned to go. It was none of their business anyway.

As fate would have it—or *was* it fate—her assigned apartment was directly across the street from Jeff's. As much as she loved the Shepherd, she still had difficulty controlling her feelings and desires for Jeff. She didn't dare talk to anyone about her sinfulness, or she would lose all status of being a True Lamb.

"Here we are!" Josie said with a squeal.

*   *   *

Jeff didn't know why he went back. Perhaps the latest batch of missionary letters prodded him. Maybe it was the jumpiness that plagued his legs, his body. He couldn't sit still. Not even for devotions. Street witnessing was out of the question.

He stepped off the bus, walking three blocks to the church. Three blocks of tormenting misery.

Go.

Don't go.

Listen, he's wise.

He's of Satan.

Stupid.

After the last visit, Reb had cornered him. "Why did you go to the pastor of that church?"

Jeff gulped, but had no guilt about what he had done. "I

148

went to defend the Flock and promote our ways to an old friend."

Reb considered a moment, rubbing his chin. He narrowed his eyes. "Because you have been so faithful to the Flock, and your work has not dwindled, I will believe you. But you'd better be careful."

Jeff's ears had burned. "How did you know I went there?"

A slow smile spread across Reb's face. "We know everything you do, Jeff Bradley."

Now, something led him up the stairs to Pastor Jim's office. Jeff was impatient. Tired. Afraid. Fighting. Nothing made sense.

He sat with his mug of coffee and, with his glare, dared Pastor Jim to say something stupid.

Jim offered him a Hershey's chocolate kiss, and popped one in his own mouth.

"How was your week, Jeff?"

Jeff continued his glare over the edge of his mug, saying nothing.

"Where have all the individuals gone, Jeff? Where is the individuality?" As he unwrapped another chocolate, he waited for an answer that did not come. After the chocolate had melted away in his mouth, Jim spoke again. "In Christianity, Jesus—or God—deals with each problem and each person in ways as varied as the person. In the Old Testament, the problems of the Jews were approached in different ways. In the New Testament, Jesus healed one blind man in stages, with mud and spit. Another time He touched a man's eyes with His fingers and the man was instantly healed. People are different, and God treats them that way."

Jeff wanted to respond with a clever retort, but he couldn't. Shep treated all males one way, all females another. He didn't want to think about that.

"Did you know God wants you to care for your body?

He created it; it's good. Its needs are not evil. You are not more holy by denying what it needs to stay healthy."

Jeff squeezed his mug. The truth of the statement nudged its way in. How could he bring people to the Flock, if he was too tired to see straight? "Every group has a few faults," he said.

"But you really don't believe the Flock has faults, do you? Especially not Shep."

Jeff looked at Jim, astonished. "Shep is perfect. There is no flaw in him."

"The Bible says, 'Any man who says he has not sinned is a fool,'" Jim quoted.

Jeff squirmed in the seat, and looked away.

"I have something I wrote out for you," Jim said. "I want you to read it and consider what it says. You are a smart young man, Jeff. You have always given your everything to Jesus. I know it is the Holy Spirit alive inside you that keeps you questioning in a group where questioning is a very evil sin. Because God is aware of your ultimate desire to serve Him, He will not let you rot in that cult."

Jim regretted his last words as soon as he said them. Jeff jumped to his feet and slammed his mug on the desk, coffee sloshing over the sides. "I am *not* rotting and the Flock is *not* a cult. And I won't be back to see you."

Jim slumped over his desk as the door slammed.

*   *   *

Deanna had never been so happy. She scrubbed and scraped years of dirt and mold off the walls, floors, and shower of her apartment. She sang songs, recited verses, and thought of the days ahead and past. It wouldn't be long now until she had a missionary assignment from Jeff. She continued preparation courses which seemed to weigh heavily on etiquette in public rather than teachings in doctrine.

One course, called the Inner Truth, taught some of the

deeper teachings of the Flock. A year ago some of the teachings might have shocked her. But now she accepted them, knowing they were all from God through Shep.

In the mornings, she worked at the main office, doing bookkeeping and financial statements. She tried to catch Jeff and find out what the holdup was on her assignment. Staff took a dim view of males and females speaking together in person about nonessential business, so she had to rely on messages sent through interoffice memos. But she never received any response to her messages. She assumed he took extra care in his planning for her.

She dreamed often of the praise Shep would shower upon her as his missionary—praise for all the new Lambs brought into the Flock.

She dipped the scrub brush into the pail of murky water. *Hah, hah, my three sisters*, she thought. *You were all first in school and in the family. But the one you looked upon as a nobody is now first in the kingdom, and in the eyes of God and His chosen prophet.*

*   *   *

Jeff stared at the envelope shoved underneath his apartment door. Lambs rarely got mail, and this had no stamp or address. Only his name. He sat on the couch before slipping his finger under the flap and ripping it open.

August 17

ARGENTINA. Before the luggage was tucked into the belly of the plane, a long coffin was shoved in place. Argentine police talked animatedly with the plane's ground crew foreman. They shoved a document into one hand, and a plastic-wrapped address label in the other. The foreman screamed until his face grew deep red, then threw his hands in the air. Passengers peering through the observation windows supposed he was about to throw the papers back at the police. Instead, he climbed into the belly of the plane, emerging moments later. Only a few passengers remarked about the odd occurrence, then forgot about it. Most didn't even notice.

WASHINGTON, D.C. The State Department was flooded with phone calls from worried families. Was the young woman their daughter, girlfriend, wife? Missionary organizations attempted to reach their outposts by ham radio. Everyone had descriptions of their loved ones; no one received any answers.

Every newsbreak on television or radio ran the top story. A mystery without answers. Was she a nun? A recent kidnap victim? A dead American in another country—perhaps a victim of terrorism. No one had the answers.

Soon, the newscasters said, they hoped to have a description of the young woman. But the plane must first land, an autopsy done, and descriptions compared.

First reports said she was blond, and many sighed or cried in relief. Next reports said she was a redhead. Nothing made sense; conflicting reports could be heard everywhere.

The plane landed. Press poured from the gates—a swarm of mosquitoes, biting where they could, sucking answers until they were temporarily satisfied.

Two State Department officials whisked the coffin away on an airport tram, under the sharp protective eyes of two security guards.

LOS ANGELES INTERNATIONAL AIRPORT. A man with dark, curly hair, and stern face, handed his ticket to the agent. His first-class ticket read: FRED ARGONSEN. *First Class.*

The agent smiled at him. "Thank you, Mr. Argonsen. Enjoy your stay in Brazil."

The man nodded but did not smile. He stood near the

window, never turning around. Another man, seated be-hind him in a plastic chair, looked as though he was read-ing a newspaper, his briefcase on the floor between his legs. A close observer could see he watched the man called Fred Argonsen at the window, as well as the people min-gling about.

When the flight was called, the seated man cleared his throat. A few moments later, only he and Fred Argonsen were left. The seated man cleared his throat twice, and Fred Argonsen turned around. They shook hands, and Fred Argonsen spoke. "Only necessary contact through agent *B* for two months. I will send for all when I prepare a place."

"Yes, Shep," the man whispered.

Shep turned and boarded the plane.

=16=

The bus heaved a large sigh, the doors flew open, and Jeff stepped off the bus behind a small gray-haired lady. "Have a nice day at the Arboretum," the bus driver called to them.

Tucking the brown paper sack underneath his arm, Jeff stuck his hand into his pocket. Three crumpled dollars paid the admission—the last of his stashed money.

He took the obligatory tram ride, without listening to the guide describe the trees and shrubs from all over the world. Instead, his eyes scanned the grounds. He noticed where most of the people wandered, and what areas they seemed to avoid.

He sucked in each breath of air. His heart thudded fast and heavy. It was all wrong. All of this. He should not be making decisions without Shep's guidance. He should not open himself up to Satan like this—but something strong compelled him.

A soft breeze tousled Jeff's curls. He stepped off the

154

tram, not noticing the pretty girl who tried to flirt with him. He put one hand on the bag under his arm to hold it still, as he walked. He walked and wandered for a long time until he found the right place.

Clusters of trees and bushes gathered together on a slope of grass. Jeff squeezed between two bushes and sat in the cool shade, hidden from the rest of the world. He dropped the heavy sack on the ground and opened it. He lifted from it his Bible, commentary, and the letter. His hand trembled, as he took the typed pages from the torn envelope.

He unfolded the letter, which had been slipped under his apartment door, then paused a moment. He looked up at the sky, without really seeing it. "God," he said quietly. "You know I've always wanted to follow You. To give my whole life to You. But everything's all mixed up now. Can You show me the truth? Is there any truth?"

His head dropped. He shut his eyes tight against the stupid tears trying to come out. What a baby he'd been lately! He pressed his lips together, his mind blank, before he opened his eyes to look at the pages scrunched in his hand.

He'd never known Pastor Jim to lie. He had other faults, other weaknesses, but he didn't lie. *But he's of Satan's world. You can't believe anything he says.*

So many times these past two weeks, Jeff had wished he could yank his brain out and throw it as far as he could. Two sides battled constantly—night and day. It didn't seem to matter if he slept or was awake. If it didn't stop soon, he'd end up in a loony bin.

He wiped his brow and wished he had thought to bring water with him. The letter before him was split into columns. One side read THE FLOCK. The other read, GOD/CHRISTIANITY. The columns showed the difference between the two. If these columns were true, then the Flock was nothing but a farce—a twisted view of the Bible.

One had to be true, the other had to be false. The more he looked at the comparisons, the more he knew that one had taken the basic truths of the other, twisted them and used them as his own: to make the truth suit his own teachings.

It made him think of the movies he used to see before joining the Flock. When you read the book, then saw the movie, you knew that somehow the best story had been distorted.

God's Word, the Bible, His story woven through Old and New Testaments, had to be the "book." The Flock had to be the "movie." Someone saw the good ideas, the truth the Bible told, and distorted it into his own message. His own salvation. Jeff had been duped to believe the distortion, the salvation of following the leader, of good works, rather than the only way God had said it would be.

> So, Jeff [the letter read], would you follow the instruction manual for a fine car, written by the person who designed and built the car, or one written by someone who had driven one like it? So many people follow counterfeits. God said, with finality, that the only way to spend eternity with Him is through His sent Messiah, Jesus. And the rest of the world says: "God couldn't possibly be so narrow-minded. You can get to Him however *you* choose."
>
> Jeff, can you get into a movie theater any other way than buying a ticket? There is only one way into a movie theater. There is only one way to eternity with God. And only one way to give birth to a relationship with Him now.

Jeff looked up from the letter and fingered a leaf that rubbed against his thigh. In the Flock, there were many ways to "join" and have eternal life. "Any method in bringing new Lambs is okay," Shep, and now Reb, said with frequency. "The end justifies the means."

Yet, Jeff wondered with surprise, once inside, there was

only one way to act, one way to be, one way to think. Jim was right. With God, there is only one way to become His child, to have that special, intimate relationship with Him. And certainly God moved in the relationship with as much individuality as the person He communicated with.

Jeff leaned back on his hands. He longed for that relationship with all his heart! To talk and be heard. To be guided with wisdom, and follow. To be filled with joy and peace, even when life hurts too much to care to go on.

I'm tired of being a clone. Just another cog in Shep's machine. Jeff slapped his hand over his mouth, as if to shut up the blasphemous words.

He quickly looked at the list again. In the Flock, Shep determined the type of work for salvation, and demanded continued work to maintain it. With God, salvation is a gift, and work flows as a result of that gift.

All that Jeff ever did arose out of a never-ending devotion to God—not out of a need to win God's approval. Jeff snorted. That was *impossible*. Who could ever hope to do enough work for God's approval? That was *absurd*.

Jeff covered his eyes. "But that's exactly what we do in the Flock," he muttered. "Witness here, work there, plant missionaries all around. And why? To earn our place in the kingdom." Jeff listened to his own words in amazement. He thought deeply in the black safety of his covered eyes. After a few moments, he felt brave enough to look at the startling paper again.

Pastor Jim's words continued to open up the dark recesses of memory in Jeff's mind. Truths Jeff had always known, but the slow twist of Shep's words had made him forget.

Jim reminded him that Jesus paid for all the wrong he had done, for all the things people do that separate them from God. The crime had to be paid for if anyone wanted to give birth to a relationship with God. And One innocent of the crime was the only one legally able to pay the required price. "Remember our study in junior high of C.S. Lewis?" Jeff read aloud. "It's like the 'deep magic' written of in the *Chronicles of Narnia*—a process written into the world before we arrived."

Jeff chewed on the inside of his cheek, remembering the anger he had stifled when he watched Shep ridicule someone who had questioned him, or levy stiff punishment for some other sin. *We pay for our own sins, in the Flock.*

Jeff began to nod as he read the next descriptions of the Flock. "There is only one human who is viewed as the final authority on Scripture, holiness and life-style—never question authority. In Christ, no human is the final authority. There are many teachers of the Bible. All can and should be questioned. Only the Bible and God are the final authority."

Inside Jeff's head, the battle raged. Jeff found himself acknowledging the truth and difference between the Flock, and God Himself. But he still defended the Flock.

A gaggle of giggles interrupted his thoughts. He froze as several kids stampeded the bushes. A little girl tripped into his hiding place. Her brown eyes grew wide, and her hand covered her open mouth. "Oohh!" she shrieked and dashed out again.

Jeff watched the leaves pop into the air wherever the kids ran. He shifted to cross his legs, and leaned to one side, reaching beneath him to toss a rock that poked him. The battle in his mind brought him back to the letter.

He flipped to the last page. He read with his jaw open. As convincing as the differences with the Bible, this was a simple discussion on how the brain actually changes its ability to function when deprived of sleep and nourishing food. Also, dumping loads of information into it, in a short amount of time, lowers the brain's ability to think critically about the information and increases susceptibility to persuasion.

Jeff shook his head, thinking of how the discussion could

have been written by someone peering through the trees at a Flock camp, or at a weekend teaching session. The author spoke, not from a religious bias, only from scientific data. *That* fact weighed heavily in his thinking.

Jeff folded the letter and put it back in the envelope. He placed it in the center of his commentary and closed the book. He moved it behind him, then lay down on it. A hard pillow. Like Jacob in the Old Testament. The story popped into his head without warning. It came from some old Sunday-school class, in which the kids acted out the story. One kid, his head on a rock for a pillow, tossed and turned. Other kids, dressed in white sheets walked up and down a ladder.

God had met Jacob in that place. Would God meet Jeff in this place?

*   *   *

Deanna stood in Jeff's office, her fingertips resting lightly on the desk in front of her. Her True Lamb smile changed to one of true delight. "It's about time!" she said.

Reb handed her a sheet of paper. "Sign and date this at the bottom."

"Okay." She signed her name. "What's the date?"

"August seventeenth."

"I should have figured it was August," she said as she printed each letter with care. "It's so hot."

She put the pen on the paper and shoved it toward him. Reb smiled at her, so pleased that the True Lambs never read what they signed. They didn't question. They were good Lambs.

"Where's Jeff?" Deanna asked.

"I was just about to ask you the same thing. We haven't seen him . . ." Reb cleared his throat ". . . all day. His, uh, roommate said he left early with a grocery bag under his arm. He watched him board the number 58 bus as he always does on his way to work." Reb yanked on a desk drawer a few times before it opened. "If you see him, tell him we want to talk to him."

"Sure." She turned to leave. She put her hand on the doorknob, then paused. "I thought all missionaries got to go overseas."

Reb looked at her sternly. "Is this a complaint?"

"Oh, no," she quickly assured him. "I *am* a bit disappointed. But I wondered why I am being sent to Washington, D.C."

"It was Jeff's decision. He convinced Shep that with your math capability, as well as your ability to get along with people, that we needed you more in Washington where you can mingle with the senators and congressmen—be their prime girl. If the Flock can touch the heart of the country, then we'll have the country."

Deanna sighed. "I suppose so. But I was looking forward to using my Spanish, or even the little French I learned."

Reb's mouth turned into one of mockery. "Your Spanish was never very good."

Deanna tried to keep her smile in place. "It would have gotten better with practice."

"Washington, D.C., is our crucial working area. If you are committed to the Shepherd, you will go where he calls."

"Thank you, Reb. I'll tell Jeff you're looking for him if I see him."

Deanna walked down the hall, her smile growing bigger with each step. Pride swelled in her, until she thought she would pop. In the past, she knew she would have been furious with Jeff for manipulating things as she knew he had. She would have yelled at Reb that her Spanish ability had nothing to do with her not being sent overseas. But now she was a good Lamb. A meek Lamb. She shouldn't even have said what little she did. But she had controlled herself and had won the victory over anger and questioning. She was a good Lamb.

*   *   *

The smell of diesel fuel wafted in through the open windows. Jeff held onto the chrome bar in front of his seat as the bus turned the corner. For the first time in a very long time, he knew what he should do, and it was the opposite of what he had been told to do.

The pain in his head pushed against his skull. He tried to sort out thoughts that would help from thoughts that would not. Nothing seemed clear except the Word of God. The last three hours he had spent reading the Bible, comparing the commentary, and the words of the Shepherd. The first two seemed right, and agreed. The third didn't.

He faced the right thing to do, and the easy thing to do. It would be easy to go back to work, to assign girls to what he now knew was a destination from which they would not return. He could stay with what he knew: the loving Family that had become his whole life; the meetings; the concerts. All of it, so comfortable, so unique. *And so wrong.*

Yet the right thing to do seemed too hard. How could he expose those he loved? Those he had and would have given his life for?

Jeff rested his chin on the bar, bumping it every time the bus jolted to a stop. Revealing the truth about someone he loved very much and had trusted so totally was a crushing option.

If he told the truth, would anyone believe him? If no one believed him, how could he go on? All the people he loved would walk away from him, choosing to believe a lie because it's safer, more comfortable. He would be left to look like a fool, and feel totally crazy.

Shep, he knew, would deny the truth to protect himself and the little world he had built up around him. To tell the truth would destroy him.

Jeff pressed his nose on the window, a surprising

thought coming to him. Maybe Shep had lived the lie for so long that now he believed it himself?

All at once he wished he'd never been born—wished he'd never heard of Parkside Presbyterian.

Maybe Shep *was* the truth and the rest of the established church was the lie. Maybe there was no truth, and God Himself was a lie—the biggest farce on the face of the earth. There is no God. There is no Messiah. All of it is a lie.

Bits and pieces of words and verses came to him. All the prophecy about the Messiah, even to the day and place of his birth—fulfilled. The method of death—fulfilled. His mother, impossibly a virgin—fulfilled. The Resurrection— must have been fulfilled. How could eleven terrified wimps, holed up in a dark room, suddenly come bursting out with confidence and eventually give their lives over to ugly deaths if the Resurrection was a lie?

Jeff wanted to stand up and scream, **So who is lying and who is telling the truth?** Instead he slumped in the seat, and waited for his stop.

With each step up the carpeted stairs, Jeff wondered what he should do. Nothing was clear in his mind. One truth against another truth. The soft music from a radio drifted in the air around him. The song's end ushered in a news bulletin. Jeff stopped, aware he had not heard the news in at least a year. He didn't know whether he should run or listen.

"The American woman found dead in Argentina yesterday is believed to be victim of a brutal beating. An anonymous call from a breathless, whispering woman stated the victim to be part of a religious group called the Flock. White slavery is suspected."

Jeff dashed up the stairs and threw open the door. "I want your help," he demanded.

$=17=$

$=$**J**eff sat nervously at his desk. He didn't know if he could go through with it. He didn't know if he could get away with it. Perhaps everyone was too preoccupied to notice. The door flew open, and Jeff started.

"Jeff, isn't it exciting?"

"Deanna!" Jeff said with surprise. "I thought you weren't speaking to me."

"Oh, no, silly. I know you are only doing the will of the Shepherd." Jeff tried not to wince. "Besides, now that everything's changed, it doesn't matter anymore."

Jeff looked confused. He hadn't been paying attention to all the activity stirring up the office the past few days. He vaguely remembered Reb coming in and talking to him about moving, but he had been too preoccupied to give it much thought. He pulled a rubber band from the drawer and popped it into his mouth. "Aren't you ready to go to Washington?"

"No. I get to go to our new paradise instead." She cocked

her head. "You don't look very excited. Everyone else can't stop talking about it."

"I guess I'm just tired," Jeff said.

"I've put tired on hold. I can't be tired thinking of all the excitement. You know, it's too bad America is going to be destroyed, of course. But God gave America a chance to turn to Him, and America ignored the true Shepherd. He will destroy America in her wickedness just as He destroyed Sodom and Gomorrah. And just as it was then, no one is to look back." Deanna spun around in a circle. "I certainly won't look back."

"Who says America is going to be destroyed?"

Deanna put her hands on her hips, looking exasperated. "Shep, of course. He says the signs are everywhere."

"What kind of signs?"

Deanna walked around the room, and began to tick them off on her fingers. "The demoralization of America—you know—no one has any moral values anymore. The turning of their backs against God and His Word. The political decay of the country."

Jeff looked amused. "And you know all these things from news reports?"

Deanna leaned against the wall. "I can't believe you. Why should I listen to news reports when I hear all I need to from Shep? I don't need to fill my mind with all the decay of America through the lying press."

Jeff chewed a moment, thinking. "What about your family, your sisters, your grandparents? What about Kathy and Linda? Aren't you afraid for them?"

For a moment, a look of panic seemed to take away some of Deanna's smile. She lifted her chin and her eyes narrowed. "No, I'm not afraid for them. They had their chance. As with the family of David and the family of Joseph, God has chosen the least to be the ruler of them all. It is not my fault they have not been chosen."

Jeff couldn't believe Deanna's arrogance. When he met

her, she had been so giving, so humble with the great gifts God had given her. Would he have been drawn to her now? His heart swelled with love for *her*—for the Deanna who never heard of the Flock. He had to get her out with him.

Jeff forced a smile. "So where is this holy paradise Shep is going to prepare for us?" he asked.

Deanna scrunched her brow together, her dark eyes confused. "I swear, Jeff, that if I didn't know you better, I'd think you were being sarcastic." She walked to the chair opposite his desk, and sat on the hard, unpainted surface. "We don't know yet. The courier just came in with a letter from Shep. It had no postmark. Sent by heavenly express, I guess!"

Jeff put his head in his hands. How could he have believed that for so long? Why didn't he guess that one envelope slipped inside another is all it takes for a letter to come bearing no postmark. He used to have a brain. Where did it go? Where had Deanna's gone?

Deanna spun around the room. "Oh, Jeff, it's so exciting."

Jeff stared at her. "Is it? Is it exciting to have no money, wear clothes that don't fit, stay up 'til midnight working hard, waking at six o'clock, never having a day off, even when you're sick?"

Deanna looked indignant. "I never get sick. All True Lambs are overcomers, and overcomers don't get sick. You know that, Jeff. What's gotten into you?"

Jeff felt a strength that didn't belong to him straighten his back and firm his resolve. "You *did* get sick, Deanna. I heard you heaving your guts in the hall bathroom here at work. Not too long after that, you had a horrendous cold and your voice was hoarse."

"That's not true, Jeff," Deanna protested, her face turning red. "I was clearing my throat in the bathroom, and I've never been sick once since I've become a True Lamb."

Jeff shook his head. "We've all become robots, Deanna.

Can't you see that? Can't you see the lies, the manipulation?"

Deanna stomped across the room to the sparse bookshelf. "Don't talk like that, Jeff Bradley, do you understand me?" She pulled a handful of Lamb Guidance booklets from the shelf. "This is my *life*, the only thing that has ever given me purpose, a reason for living. Before, I felt like I was always falling through the cracks of society. Now I am more valuable than everyone else. Don't you understand that?"

Jeff hung his head. He didn't understand that. The whole reason *he* had followed Shep was because he wanted to follow Jesus, and he mistakenly thought Shep would lead the way. His head snapped up. "Deanna, come with me. I'll give you a reason for living. You will be special to me. You won't be last among sisters; you will be first, as a wife."

Deanna dropped the books, stunned. "Are you leaving, Jeff?" she whispered. "Do you know what happens to people who leave the Flock? Their lives are destroyed; Satan gobbles them up." She covered her face. "There is no hope, only horror waiting them."

Jeff strode over to her, pulling her hands from her face. "Satan is gobbling us up, here in the Flock. America won't be destroyed. That's just another lie. Another ploy for you to follow Shep wherever and whatever he does."

Deanna yanked her hands from Jeff's loving grasp. "*You're* the lie, Jeff. America *will* be destroyed."

"You said you haven't listened to the news lately, right?" Jeff asked cautiously.

"Of course not. That's against Lamb Guidelines." She took on a look that reminded Jeff of Josie. "You haven't been listening to the news either, have you?"

Jeff dragged her to a chair and sat her down in it. He knelt in front of her. "Deanna, I know you won't listen to me now. But if I tell you this, I hope it will sink in and you will hear it before it's too late. There are some bad things happening. Shep's been found out, and he knows it."

"What do you mean he's been *found out?*" Deanna hated the spinning and fear that began to seep inside.

"I can't tell you yet. It's time for the Shepherd to move on. If he doesn't, it could mean prison."

Deanna leaned back. "I don't believe you, Jeff Bradley. Satan's gotten hold of your brain, but good." Her eyes took on a glazed look, and she began chanting one verse, over and over. Jeff walked away, feeling defeated. How could he expect her to believe him? Shep represented all holiness— Jeff a mere hopeless sinner. All at once he spun around, went to Deanna and shook her shoulders until the glazed look left her eyes. He stared straight into her eyes and said, "You shall know the truth and the truth shall set you free. John, chapter eight, verse thirty-two, Deanna. I started praying that verse, that God would give me the truth."

"And He told you that the truth in Shep is a lie? His own called one is some sort of bad man? Oh, Jeff. I'm not staying here anymore. I've got some phone calls to make and figures to work up to give Reb for the cost of sending us to paradise."

As Deanna marched across the room, Jeff called after her. "Deanna, please pray that verse and mean it—just once, okay?"

Deanna hesitated at the door, without turning around. Jeff quickly quoted again. "You shall know the truth and the truth shall set you free." The door opened, Deanna disappeared behind a slam that made Jeff shudder.

Jeff closed his eyes and shook his head, sinking into the chair. What monstrous thing had he done? Not only had he let himself get sucked in, but he also brought with him the one he cared about most.

He took a deep breath and shuffled through all the papers he had kept in secret places. He started working faster and faster, suddenly realizing Deanna could report him to Reb at any second. He slapped his hand to his forehead. How stupid! He should never have said anything to Deanna here, in his office. He had no idea who was listening.

He took one brief moment to look around, then began to take anything he thought might help the police. He shoved everything into different pockets so it wouldn't look like any pockets bulged. He took the largest Lamb Guidance book, and put a few more papers into it.

He looked with sadness around the stark room. Like Deanna, he had found acceptance here too. He had found a purpose, when life had neglected to give him any before. He felt himself weaken. Why should he leave? What else mattered but finding a place in the world?

He sat back down at his desk. He opened the center drawer and looked at the pen and pencil lying neatly in their tray. A small box of paper clips sat to one side. On the other, a rubber stamp with the address of the office building resting on top of a tin containing the ink pad. A yellow lined pad of paper centered in the drawer. This was home, how could he leave? Jeff opened the side drawer, containing all the files, once more. He pulled the secret papers from the hiding places in his pants and windbreaker. He moved the files forward and stopped. Reaching in, he pulled on a corner of a white paper that stuck out between some files. He tugged gently. Whatever it was wouldn't budge. Jeff stuck his other hand in to unjam it. He pulled out a photograph. Deanna. On the back listed her first name, age, hair color, and so on. His mind flashed to other photographs of girls he knew would never come back.

Jeff left amid the shouts and chanting of his family:

LOVE SHALL RULE, YEAH, YEAH, YEAH. LOVE SHALL RULE.

Jeff shouted with them, changing the chant to:

SHEP SHALL RULE, YEAH, YEAH, YEAH. SHEP SHALL RULE.

Deanna watched Jeff through the open door of the office where she worked. She heard him chant and cheer, she saw the genuine smile light his face. Something seemed odd about his smile, until she realized it had been a long time since she had seen him smile like that. Most of the time, his smile stretched across his lips without being sincere. This time, it took over his whole face.

She put her mind to her work. Charter flight costs to Brazil, Africa, and Bolivia. She wondered where they would go. Top secret plans. They wouldn't know until they boarded the plane. She tried to keep her mind in focus, but it didn't seem to want to stay there. Jeff's words had popped holes in her confidence. Each time they came up, she stifled them by chanting a verse. How thankful she was to have all those Bible verses at her disposal. She could always use them to fight off the enemy.

Reb came in and Deanna looked up at him. "Why the long look, Deanna? Where is the joy of our Shepherd who will save us from the destruction of America?" His words seemed to conflict with the searching look on his face. He seemed to be looking into her very soul, probing into the private places in her heart and mind. Deanna looked away, trying not to squirm.

She slowly and deliberately showed him some preliminary figures. "There is no way we can transport all the Southern California Flock, wherever we are going, not to mention the Midwest and East Coast Flocks. The funds simply aren't available."

Reb smiled broadly. He seemed relieved about something. "Deanna, the Lord provides. Besides, we have a special campaign that is sure to bring in enough to fly us all to paradise."

"What's that?" Deanna asked, her smile returning.

"Most of the Lambs have parents. Most parents love their Lambs."

"But we have left them for our new family."

"That's right. But families tend to hold on long past the time to let go. Each of you will ask your parents for seven hundred dollars to build a shelter for abandoned children. Whatever we can get from them will be fine. We can make up the rest from other funds you haven't seen yet."

"Reb, that's lying," Deanna said softly.

Reb looked disappointed. "Deanna," Reb scolded gently. "You know that all methods are holy when the outcome is righteous." He messed up her hair.

Deanna watched him go, and returned to her figures. Before Jeff had talked to her, she would have let the matter drop, knowing Reb was right. But now, ugly doubts pestered her. She hated Jeff for doing that evil to her.

She put her mind to the task, working fervently far into the night. She grabbed a stale doughnut from one of the secretary's desks. People all around her shredded documents by hand, making decisions over what was important to keep, what must be destroyed, and what must be packed.

At ten, the frenetic activity continued. Jerry ran through the office waving a stack of papers. "We've got the office leased, and all the equipment sold!" A cheer rose from the busy Lambs, and songs burst forth, encouraging them on.

One number began to look like another to Deanna's blurry eyes. She rubbed her eyes, shook her head, and tried again. She could not let up, for they had to leave the day after tomorrow. Reb said the destruction was coming soon, and they must get out.

Starting at eleven, all over the room, phone calls were made. Each person who had parents called them, begging money for their shelter. The parents were told the Flock had sixteen abandoned children suddenly left in their care, and they must provide a place for them, or they would be turned over to the state. "And Mom, Dad, you would never let that happen to a poor child, would you?"

One girl broke down on the phone, realizing she would never see her parents again. Her parents, thinking her tears were for the poor children, offered double the amount requested. When she hung up the phone, Samuel slapped her cheek and demanded, "Girl, do you want to be a True Lamb or not?"

The girl nodded.

"Then denounce the evil, satanic family that has you in its grip." He paused, looking at her tear-streaked face, which angered him even more. "Denounce them, *now!*"

A tiny voice came from her. "I denounce them," she said, without any conviction evident at all.

Samuel's face grew red, his shoulders squared as he slapped her again. "You must denounce them and proclaim your loyalty to the Shepherd. I would kill my own family if the Shepherd asked me to. Now let me hear where your true loyalty lies."

The girl gulped. "I denounce my family, born of the sinful flesh, and their denial of the true Shepherd. I will leave them for the righteousness only the Shepherd can give."

The group cheered at the word-perfect proclamation all had given at their True Lamb ceremony. Samuel smiled. "For you to remember that oath must mean you are truly sincere in your declaration." He slapped her on the behind. "Go, now, little one, and remain true to him who loves you enough to lay down his life for you."

The whole scenario made Deanna's head spin. The girl deserved the slaps, the punishment for her sin. So why did the usual, common way of doing things, suddenly make her stomach turn upside down?

It's that awful Jeff and his lying words. She slammed down her pencil and marched to Reb's door, calling, "Reb, I've got to talk to you about something important. Right now!"

= 18 =

=Deanna hesitated to open the door without being invited in. She really wasn't allowed to speak with him. As her thoughts swarmed over her, she forgot even to knock. She formed her words carefully in her head. "Reb," she decided she would say, "I've got a report on a Lamb who might be turning from the Truth."

Before her words could tumble out, she heard Reb's angry voice. She stopped, the door open only a crack, her heart jumping in her chest.

"Are you sure, *very sure* you saw him with the police?" Reb kicked his booted feet up on the desk. "So why didn't you stop him? I told you to keep strict tabs on him. *Now* where is he?" Reb's feet flew to the ground as he jumped up. "You lost him? You are going to pay for this, and you are going to pay dearly. I don't want any of the other Lambs to know about this. We'll have to speed up the process. I wish you weren't such an imbecile!" The receiver slammed in the cradle, startling Deanna. Reb sat heavily in his chair, running angry fingers through his hair.

She was about to flee, when Reb punched out some numbers on the phone. He muttered something, then anger raised his voice. "Yeah, he was trying to talk his girl into leaving. . . ." Reb chuckled and lifted his voice to a falsetto. "Oh, Deanna," he mimicked cruelly, "come with me, I'll give you a reason for living."

Deanna felt her whole life sink to a big hole in the middle of her. She couldn't listen any more.

Deanna closed the door behind her. In the hallway, Samuel leaped toward her, and Deanna jumped back, sucking in a startled, "Oh!"

"Isn't it great," he said, grabbing her around the waist. "In two days, we'll be serving our Shepherd in the earthly kingdom. All of us will take our rightful spots and serve him forever."

Deanna stood tall and stiff, too frightened to move. Samuel danced off down the hall, and Deanna ran to the bathroom. She locked the door and leaned against it.

You shall know the truth and the truth shall set you free.

I took vows. I did. I was proud of those vows, willing to fulfill them.

Then why are you afraid?

"It isn't right," she said out loud, then covered her mouth.

It IS right, her mind pleaded. *Jeff is wrong. Whatever the Shepherd ordains is right and good. So there must be something wrong with me. I must not be as holy as I thought. Oh, God, oh, Shepherd, forgive me for not being holy and willing to accept your will.*

Deanna washed her face with cold water and went back to her desk. She stacked her papers, attaching adding machine tapes to the appropriate reports. As she finished, Reb came in.

"Okay, what is it you wanted to report?"

Deanna stared at him, not knowing what to say.

* * *

Jeff felt weak from his hours at the police station. His documents did not prove enough to arrest Shep, and possibly Reb, because the identity of the dead girl had not yet been established.

His knowledge of Shep before he became the Shepherd was important to the police, in case something should tie in. Jeff discovered that the Mitch Campbell who led the youth group at Parkside Presbyterian, was neither Shep nor Mitch Campbell. His real name was Fred Argonsen. That's all they knew right now.

And all Jeff knew, was that he was scared. Very scared. If Shep ever found out who had given the information, he would be dead.

Pastor Jim put his arm around Jeff's shoulders for a moment. "You have done a very brave thing, Jeff. Let me take you home."

Jeff looked at Jim. "Home. That sounds so odd." As he let himself into Jim's car, he said, "I'm a little frightened of home, Jim. The whole world seems so off-balance."

Jim started the car. "It will for a while, I'm afraid."

It was as if Jeff was seeing his house for the first time. It looked large, and expensive. Jim sped off as Jeff walked up the steep, narrow, cement steps. The ivy dripped over the walls, flowers cheered the patch of dirt on top of the wall.

Jeff felt awkward knocking on the door. He would have felt even more awkward just walking in. His father opened the door, the soft light from some back room spilling out. Before he realized what was happening, his father had him in a bear hug. "Jeff! I have missed you. How are you? What are you doing home? I thought you were too busy to come see an old man like me."

Jeff hung his head, then looked straight at his father. "I've left the Flock, Dad."

"Oh!" his father said, putting his arm around Jeff's shoulder and drawing him into the house. "I see."

Jeff's mother came floating down the hall. "Jeff, honey, how come you're home?" She gave him a light lipstick kiss on his cheek.

"Jeff's left the Flock, Melinda."

"No, go on!" Jeff's mother checked her son out in disbelief.

"Yes, Mother, I have. And I wondered if I could have my old room back for a month or so until I can get a job and find a new place."

"Well . . . well . . ." his mother stuttered. She began to tremble, putting her hand up to her mouth. Suddenly, her hand dropped, her face contorted with anger. "*No.* No you can't stay, Jeff. You have . . . have promised something to Shep and you must fulfill it. Why he has been the best parent to you! You can't be ungrateful to him now."

Jeff's father put his arm around his wife's shoulders, holding on until her skin turned a bloodless white beneath his fingers. "Of course you can stay, son. You look beat. Go take a shower and hop into that bed. I'll make sure your mother has put clean sheets on it."

As Jeff lay on the bed, overfatigued and unable to sleep, the door opened slowly. He looked up to see his mother looking pale and fragile in the soft light.

"Can I come in?"

Jeff got up on one elbow. "Of course, Mom."

She sat on the very edge of his bed, reached her hand out as if she planned to touch him, then placed it next to her on the rough spread. Jeff couldn't remember ever seeing his mother so frightened. She picked at the spread, her mouth working at forming the words that wouldn't come.

"If . . . if what you say is true, then, then. . . ." She put her hands to her face, as tears began to pour down her cheeks.

Jeff sat up, leaning forward and hugging her. "It's okay, Mom."

Jeff's mother pulled back from the hug. "It's not okay, Jeff. You don't know. You just don't know."

Jeff stared at her in bewilderment, speechless.

She wiped her tears and continued crying. "Jeff, I love you so much. I've worried so about Shep, ever since that meeting with the other parents. But how could I say anything to you? How could Shep be anything but good?"

"Mom," Jeff interrupted tenderly, and then he didn't know what else to say.

"Jeff, don't you see?" she pleaded. "I've looked to Shep as the parent I could not be for you. You needed so much intelligence and wisdom that I lacked. You had a strong spirit that I didn't know how to handle. I felt a man, a godly man, would give you all that you needed. If you come home. . . ." She buried her face in her hands. Again, her cheeks flooded with tears.

Jeff had never seen his mother as anything but a tower of strength, a socialite who had all the answers, all the proper ways to act. He never knew, never imagined that she might be terrified . . . of *him*!

"Mom, don't worry anymore. I won't stay long. I won't trouble you."

She looked at him with weary eyes. "Oh honey. . . ." She stood and left the room.

It was a long time before Jeff fell into a fitful sleep.

The morning sun brought more turmoil.

"I still don't understand how you can say Shep has done wrong," his mother repeated for the tenth time. "That man is the most holy man I've ever met."

"I'm not real sure I understand either, Mom. Along with the information I have gathered, there are also the suspicious ways he's been acting."

Melinda lifted her china coffee cup, with trembling

hands, to her pale lips. "Suspicious?" she asked in a whisper.

"He has been out of the country many times this past year. He has been gone for at least a month now. He has never before left us for so long."

"Sure," she said, her voice a mere shadow of its usual luster. "He must go tend to his other Lambs. He is a holy man. His services are needed everywhere."

"Mom. I can't stay anymore," Jeff said, placing his empty mug down as the period at the end of his sentence.

Melinda took her fragile cup to the sink. She seemed small and fragile herself, wrapped in her peach satin robe. "Maybe you shouldn't stay here, either. I'd hate to see you act this way over some imagined little offense."

Jeff shook his head, wondering if he had dreamed her coming to his room the night before. "Mom, it isn't some imagined little offense. It is a real crime he has committed."

She leaned over the sink, as if her shoulders carried a weight too heavy for her petite form. "Don't you *ever* let me hear you say something against Shep again, do you hear me?" she said, her voice straining at words she didn't seem to want to say. "And you won't stay here another night. You are to go back with Shep and ask for forgiveness for misunderstanding him."

Jeff took his mug to the sink and put his arm around her shoulder. "I love you, Mom." He left his breakfast untouched and his mother crying.

He went to his room, and made the bed. He picked up his backpack, stuffed with the few things he could get from his apartment that would not arouse suspicion in his roommate.

An envelope stuck out of the top. When Jeff saw his father's writing, he decided to read it later. He shoved it down inside, and with long strides, went out the front door and down to the street. He shook his head and bounded back up the stairs.

He stuck his head inside the door and called, "Mom?" He waited and there was no answer. "Mom? Can I at least have a dollar for bus fare?"

He could hear her sigh all the way from the kitchen. She came out, coin purse in hand. She grabbed a bunch of change and dumped it into his outstretched hand. She turned and moved away without saying good-bye.

"Thanks, Mom," Jeff said quietly. She paused a moment, then went on without turning around.

In Pastor Jim's office, Jeff pounded his fists on the sides of his head. "What am I going to do?"

"Will your father help you?"

Jeff sat up. "Wait a sec." He reached inside the backpack and retrieved the letter. He tore it open and read the short note.

> Dear Son,
> I'm sorry your mother can be so stubborn. Here is some money I hope will get you started in your new life. Call me when you get settled, or if you need some more help. I have some connections with people who could use a smart young man like you.
>   Love, DAD

Jeff looked at the check, made out to him for two thousand dollars. He put his head on Jim's desk, feeling much like a sissy for all the tears.

*   *   *

"Would you settle down and go to sleep?" Josie called to Deanna from the bedroom. "You're driving me nuts."

Deanna paced. Back and forth across the living room, into the kitchen and out again. Around and around the one chair.

Josie stood at the doorway, leaning against it, her hair smushed up. "What's the problem, Deanna?"

"Nothing, Josie. Just so excited about our move, I can hardly wait."

"Then why aren't you all packed? We leave in the morning."

"I know, Josie, I know."

Deanna plopped on the couch, her left leg bouncing up and down on her right knee. "Why are we going, Josie?"

"A True Lamb never questions."

Deanna bit her finger. "It just seems weird, that's all."

Josie stood with her hands on her hips. "Well I'm not going to question the Word of God. I'm not going to be so haughty as to think I know better than God. I'm going to obey."

"Josie," Deanna said quickly. "Haven't you ever been, um, you know, scared of the future?"

"Never. Is that what's bugging you?"

Deanna moved uncomfortably. "I guess."

Josie tipped her head back and laughed, then sat next to Deanna. She picked up Deanna's hand and held it in hers. "Deanna, nothing is scary in God's kingdom. All is pure and holy. Actually, I look forward to it. I look forward to serving God in any way and anywhere I can."

She slapped Deanna's hand lightly, and stood up. "If that's all you're afraid of, you can just forget it and come to bed."

Deanna forced a smile. "Okay. I'll come to bed in a couple of minutes. I think I'll have a glass of water."

Josie disappeared, and Deanna went to the kitchen. As she turned on the water, she prayed her first undictated prayer since the first night of camp. "God. Jeff has mixed me all up. I'm supposed to leave for Your earthly kingdom tomorrow. Please show me the truth, and set me free from all this confusion. I know the truth will be the Shepherd chosen by You. But make it real clear, okay?"

She poured the water out without drinking it and went to bed.

*   *   *

The word came across the wire. The American girl found in Argentina was Debbie Chapman. Her parents were notified. In their grief, they could not remember where the office was located that sent her to Argentina. As a matter of fact, they had never known where it was. The whole thing had happened so quickly, and they didn't even know she had left until they had received a letter.

Well, yes, they knew the name of the group, but the police would have to excuse them. Perhaps they could come back in the morning after the Chapmans had adjusted some to the shock. No, they couldn't answer any more questions.

The police paced their floors, the captain shouted questions. They decided a few more hours wouldn't make that much difference anyway.

= 19 =

= Jeff saw her face over and over. Debbie Chapman. Little Debbie—Deanna had been so jealous of her. Little Debbie who relied on him for hugs. Debbie who had been so excited about being a missionary.

The media wasn't kind. They spared no details. The whole of America knew exactly what kind of life she had to have been living. Her body proved it—but they didn't know what Jeff knew: that she had not entered into that life-style of her own wishes. She had done her holy duty.

It came as little relief that Jeff himself hadn't made the assignment. How many assignments had he made in six months? Thirty? Sixty? Even one would have been too many.

He wandered around his new apartment, not knowing what to do with himself. Every day for the past year, he had been told what to do and when to do it. He automatically followed the morning and evening schedule his first day. But what should he do in between morning and evening? Should he look for a job? How would he go about looking for one?

He lifted the rainbow-striped curtains in the bedroom, staring at the gas station below. The world seemed a strange and forbidden place with rules he didn't understand or know how to follow.

He searched the streets for a man in a suit, smoking, and idly looking about. The last he had seen of him was the day he went to the police. He shivered in the warm air. They must be planning something. They must know where he was.

He refused to tell Pastor Jim about it. He didn't want Jim to think he was flipping out and becoming paranoid, imagining things and people that didn't exist. He leaned his head on the windowpane, wondering if this was part of Shep's plan—to make him crazy by having him tailed every minute of the day, and then stop abruptly. *Well, Shep. It's working.*

He wandered into the living room and sat on the couch. Jim had rustled it up from some dark closet with incredible speed. As a matter of fact, all of the furniture, and most of the kitchen necessities had been donated from someplace or another. Probably everything came from Parkside Church members, who had no idea whom they gave to. Would they have given them to a crazy person? A follower of a Shepherd?

Jeff looked around. His new apartment wasn't much better than his last. The furnishings were just as sparse, just as threadbare, just as dusty. It felt very odd to be alone. It felt even more odd not to have people knocking at his door, or just walking right in at any time of the day or night. No one to tell him when to eat, when to go to bed, when to shower or shave. He never felt this lost with Shep. He was the good Shepherd who knew what the Lambs needed and when. There was nothing Jeff wanted more than to go back.

If he went back, there would be retribution for his crimes against the Shepherd and the Flock. The only question was who would be chosen to measure it out to him—and when. And if he didn't go back, there would still be retribution, only worse.

Long, slow footsteps approached his door, stopped. A heavy hand knocked. Jeff gulped, his fears breaking into sweat. The knock came again. Jeff decided he might as well get it over with.

He turned the knob and came face-to-face with a police officer. "Jeff Bradley?"

"Yes, sir."

"We need you at the station for more questioning. Right away."

"I have nothing more to say," Jeff said, beginning to close the door.

The officer stuck his arm straight out, holding the door open. He stared at Jeff. "You don't have the option to refuse. I thought you wanted to stop this person from continuing to send women into slavery."

Jeff winced. He looked to the ground and pulled his shoulders together. "You don't understand," he said softly.

"What?"

Jeff looked up. "I don't have a car, sir."

"We'll take you."

Jeff took three steps to his kitchen counter and slid the apartment key into the palm of his hand. Seen twice with the police. His doom was sealed, and he knew it.

*   *   *

Deanna took the army duffel bag assigned to her, threw it in the bus, and climbed in after it. All the Lambs laughed and sang, hugging each other over and over. They didn't care that the neighboring apartment buildings had windows filled with gawkers.

Three yellow school busses shut their doors, like Noah

and his ark, separating the redeemed from the doomed. Cheers filled the air; excitement filled the hearts.

Deanna bit her lip. She had sworn she wouldn't look back, and she didn't. But she couldn't keep her thoughts from looking back.

When they did, they seemed twisted and distorted. As though the house in La Crescenta had been a fuzzy dream. Her family, a story she heard long ago in a thick book of fairy tales. Her school. Her friends. Jeff.

Josie poked her ribs and smiled, clapping and singing a Victory for the Shepherd chorus. Deanna smiled in return, picked up the beat and sang with all her heart.

*   *   *

Jeff spent two hours all but refusing to talk to the police. They tried every trick they knew to get him to tell them things he didn't want to say. They used names, places, photographs, and addresses to prod him. Each word he spoke flopped his insides around. He didn't want to do this to his friends, his *family*.

He sat for a long time, listening to questions, and shaking his head at the answers. He didn't look at anyone, only the table etched with years and names of people previously interrogated there.

The tall, blond captain patted him on the back. "We've been rough on you, Jeff. We'll take you home, and maybe you can come again tomorrow and answer some more questions."

Jeff nodded numbly. *I won't be here tomorrow,* he thought. "I don't need a ride home. I'll take a bus."

"Are you sure?"

"Yeah, thanks."

Jeff walked down the street, not noticing the run-down shops he passed. His thoughts combed through the last five years of his life with the Shepherd. First as Mitch Campbell, then as Shep, after the vision.

They had been good years. Years filled with direction.

Fun years. Years at camp, learning, playing, becoming a kid again. The times Shep had put his arm around him and led him into the Truth. The times he'd been rebuked, and punished when he'd deserved it.

There was no place in the world like the Flock.

Something caught his eye. The date. The time. The temperature. The digital board on the roof of the bank flickered through the routine.

Today, Jeff thought, *the plane leaves for the earthly kingdom. To be with Shep in a new world, with a new job.* He smiled to himself. *And to be with Deanna.* He had to make his decision now. There would be no turning back, not ever.

It was as if his vision cleared.

One phone call, a question to a bus driver, and he was gone to the airport. Just like that. Maybe he could make a good, intelligent decision based on the whole picture after all.

*   *   *

Jeff ran through the concourse, his unused muscles screaming from the pressure to go faster. He hoped his information gathered from the agent at the front desk was correct, pleading with God that it was correct. The right gate, the right departure time. He knew the plane would leave early. He knew it in his heart. *Oh, God, please don't let me be late.*

People smiled as he passed, some telling their companions about the time they almost missed their flight.

He pressed on, his goal, the most important thing, just ahead.

*   *   *

Deanna chatted with Josie and Carol, each fluttery about their first international flight, and first view of the insides of a jumbo 747.

"Well, Lambs," Reb's smooth voice came from behind Deanna. "Are you ready for paradise?" He asked all three, but seemed to be looking at Deanna for the answer.

"Oh, yes, Reb," Carol and Josie crooned.

Deanna gulped, and put on her best smile. "It's going to be marvelous, isn't it Reb?"

Reb continued to look at Deanna, his face twitching. "I want to talk with you a moment, Deanna."

Josie and Carol politely walked away, leaving Deanna with Reb, whose face grew stern. "Where is Jeff?" he demanded.

"I don't know."

Reb grabbed her upper arm, leading her roughly away from the group. "You do know, and I want you to tell me."

Deanna's face grew white. "I really don't know, Reb. Why?"

Reb's grip grew tighter on Deanna's arm. "If you know, and are covering for him. . . ."

Tears of pain filled Deanna's eyes. "I am loyal to the Shepherd, Reb. I would tell you if I knew."

Reb's probing eyes searched her all over as if she hid the information somewhere inside her old dress.

"Has he done something wrong?"

Reb threw her arm down and walked away, muttering to himself. "I've told Shep, Manheim was only a stupid idiot. Can't even follow a simple tail. Loses the most important. . . ."

Deanna shivered, the tears spilling over. She hoped their flight would save Jeff from Shep's wrath, no matter what Jeff had done.

The agent announced over the speaker, that the plane was ready to board. The Lambs stood and cheered, and rushed to be the first.

Caught in the milling crowd, Deanna felt crushed. At once, she felt a strong, firm hand on hers. A man's hand, pulling her to the side. She couldn't see him over the tall Lambs around her.

It's Reb. He's got another question for me. I wish he'd leave me alone.

When she saw the strange man's face, she gasped, then squirmed, trying to get loose. Before she could yell, he had pulled her, running away from the group.

"Let go!" she said loudly, but went unheard by the cheering, singing Lambs.

"Jeff needs to talk to you," the man said. She suddenly realized that his face was kind and concerned.

"Is he coming? Is Jeff coming?" Deanna asked, excited that he had changed his mind. Maybe Reb would be lenient. Jeff's smile two nights before *had* been one of return to the Flock. He wouldn't deny the Shepherd. He would be with her in the kingdom.

"Yes, he's coming," the man said. "He wants to talk to you."

"Of course," Deanna said.

* * *

The plane took off ninety minutes ahead of the stated schedule. The flight attendants had never served such a boisterous group of young people on a charter flight. They were not interested in the offered movie or earphones. They preferred instead to sing campfire songs, religious songs, to chant verses, and shout cheers.

To their amazement, the passengers even broke into groups and began to have competitions in the aisles.

The plane landed nine hours later in a land where spring was just beginning. Spring, a time of warmth, a new growth, casting off the cold of winter. Springtime, a time when the Flock would begin to live in their Kingdom of Joy.

The plane taxied to the far end of the terminal building. The door opened, and a gasp followed by a cheer greeted the man dressed in a robe of royal blue.

"Shep!"

"It's our Shepherd!"

"Oh, Shep! We've missed you!"

The Shepherd held up his arms, and the Lambs were

silent. "This is the land where we will build our hopes. America has turned her back on God and will be destroyed. The other planes have already landed. The workers, the True Lambs, are eager to meet you. Our work here, as one Flock, is only begun. Let us rejoice in our work to be done in our new country."

The joyful crush of Lambs leaving the plane jammed the aisles.

Josie stretched. "I wonder what new and glorious work we will be able to do here for our Shepherd. It must be special if God would lead us all the way here."

Carol nodded. "Maybe now we can live in the freedom of our own community we've always longed for."

"I hope so." Josie looked around. "You know, Carol, this plane is so big I still haven't seen Deanna."

"She probably found Jeff." Carol stepped into the aisle. "I don't know, Josie. But sometimes I think Deanna would still give everything for Jeff instead of Shep."

"Oh, no, Carol. You've got Deanna all wrong. She is totally devoted to the Shepherd. Always will be."

*　　*　　*

Jeff put his arm around Deanna. She hung onto him, a frightened bird in the cover of a mighty wing. They walked slowly, both uncertain about the choice they had made. Was it right? Was it holy? Was there a right and true and holy anything in the world? Or was everything built on a bed of deceit and evil?

The Shepherd. They had looked up to him and trusted him as a spiritual father. He had seemed to be a loving, caring father. One who had time for them. One who listened, who gave guidance. They had thought it was concern that made him care enough to set limits on them, set boundaries that could not be shaken. They never suspected boundaries could be borne out of a man hungry for power, and fearful his power would be taken away if there were no boundaries.

They could not deny the good they had felt from being a part of the Flock. They could not deny the total giving sacrifice of themselves to the Flock. It was a part of Deanna's last two years, and the last five years of Jeff's life. It was too much to give up. Besides, they both wondered, perhaps all truth carries with it some falsehood.

As they walked along, they tried in vain to shut out the airport noise. Many happy voices contrasted with the struggle they had inside.

The bright sunshine of the world outside promised a new beginning. It wouldn't be easy. Some might think it would be all fun now. Some would think it a time for rejoicing, a time for soaring like an eagle. Things had changed; the old shackles had been cast off. The whole world stretched out ahead of them. A new world.

Jeff opened the door for Deanna. She slid into the front seat and Jeff slid in next to her.

Jim started the car, then turned to look at them. "You have done a hard and brave thing."

Jeff stared out the window. "It was hard; I don't know if it was brave."

Fat tears rolled down Deanna's face. "I want to go to the Shepherd."

"Do you *really* Deanna? After all the proof I've shown you?" Jeff asked, tenderly, and fully wondering if he had made the right decision himself.

Deanna shook her head. She twisted the hem of her worn dress in her hands and looked at Jeff. "How could he, Jeff? How could he do such an awful thing?" She continued to cry. "He *used* us, Jeff. He lied to me and used me."

Jeff held her shoulder tighter. "And then he changed God's words to make us follow him. He stole God's right to be called our Father."

"Shep taught me to pray, to trust, to believe my life had

a greater purpose than I ever imagined. That's not fair, Jeff. Where will I ever find someone like that again?"

Pastor Jim cleared his throat softly, not sure he should speak up. "You can still pray, trust, and *know* your life has a greater purpose than you can imagine. God promises that. Your focus needs only to change from Shep to God."

"Pastor Jim," Deanna said hesitantly, the name unfamiliar to her, "do you expect me to trust you? I've given all my trust . . . my whole *life* to this man. How can I trust you, or even God, anymore?"

Jim reached his hand out the window and paid the parking fee. "I don't expect you to trust me, Deanna. It will be a long, long time before you can trust anyone again. With Jeff as your friend, you can explore trust together."

Deanna looked at Jeff. He looked haggard and scared. She turned back to Jim. "Jeff is the only person I think I can trust." She leaned her head on the back of the seat. "Jeff, where do we go from here?"

Jeff continued to gaze out the window as if he didn't hear her. After a long moment, he breathed, "I don't know."

Jim sighed. "I can't imagine how difficult this is for you two. But I'm willing to be with you to help as long as you need me." He smiled. "I will also continue to pray for you."

Deanna looked confused. *"Continue* to pray?"

Jim's smile took over his whole face. "I started praying for you both the minute Jeff called me the first time. I haven't stopped praying for you to see the truth, and to be free of the lies Shep told you, Deanna."

Deanna returned a weak smile. "That means a lot to me. You know, I don't think Shep ever really prayed for us as individuals. All his prayers were for what we could do for him as a group." Deanna's voice became bitter. "And to think I always wanted to belong to a group. Look where *that* got me."

Jeff looked away from the world outside his window, saying nothing. He shifted to hold Deanna's hand. He began to massage it gently. "We asked for the truth, Deanna."

The somber look returned to Deanna's face. "The truth hurts."

Jeff bit his bottom lip and closed his eyes.

Jim maneuvered the car in and out of the slow traffic. He didn't know where he would take them.

Deanna rubbed her temples with her fingertips. "My mind is mush, Jeff."

Jim patted her knee. "It will feel that way for a while. The methods of the Flock altered your brain's patterns and affected your personality. It will take a long time for that to heal."

Jeff leaned forward to better see Jim's face. "Did they really do that?"

Jim nodded. "Remember the secular study I gave you on how cults work? I'm afraid that the processes they discussed are identical to what Shep used. Long meetings, with too much information. Low food intake coupled with high sugar content and lack of sleep. Peer-group pressure, denial of bodily needs, and control by the leader of every minute actually do something to the chemical processes in the brain. Once the brain is altered, it's a long, slow journey of healing."

"Maybe it's not possible for healing to happen," Deanna said suddenly.

"It is your choice."

Jeff continued to softly massage her hand, more for his comfort than for hers. "With God nothing is impossible . . . you will know the truth, and the truth will set you free."

A feeling of peace seemed to fill the ache Deanna had always carried with her. What did belonging to a group matter, if you belonged to the God of the universe? In the airport, Jeff had showed her in the Bible that God accepted her and loved her as an individual. God didn't turn people away because they belonged or didn't belong to a certain group. A tiny smile played about Deanna's mouth. She looked up at Jeff. The dancing light in her eyes had returned. "We are free, aren't we?"

Jeff leaned down and kissed her on the forehead, feeling as if he broke a law to do so. And it felt great. "I guess so, Deanna."

He rolled down the window and let the cool wind rush over him. They would heal, he and Deanna. He had no doubts anymore.